Footprints

Anna Wigley

gomer

First impression – 2004

ISBN 1 84323 277 4

This book is published with the financial support
of the Welsh Books Council.

*Printed in Wales at
Gomer Press, Llandysul, Ceredigion SA44 4QL*

Contents

PRINCE

My cousin Jack kept birds. I don't mean budgies or canaries, or anything you could put in a cage. He kept falcons. He'd fallen in love with them when he was fourteen years old and my aunt and uncle took him to the hawking centre. It was a place on the wild coast of North Wales, and I think he was enchanted by the whole thing: the landscape, the bearded burly man who ran the centre, and the atmosphere of strictness mixed with fantasy that prevailed there. Here was his first real sight of what an education meant: not the routine sarcasm and contempt of his teachers at school, who branded him a dreamer because he spent lessons staring out of the window; but a way of being grown up, a discipline that was at the same time a thing of joy and glory. He had not known till then what learning meant.

And of course there were the birds. On that first visit, he watched a peregrine falcon being flown. A young girl flew him – the owner's daughter – and Jack never forgot her small, slight figure, dressed in shabby corduroys and a baggy, man's jacket, standing with such quiet authority in the July sun, her gloved hand holding the magnificent bird like a great torch whose flame might prove dangerous. He recalled the deft, busy way she had with her hands. She would gather the leather leash, clenching her wrist and fist under the bird's iron feet that occasionally adjusted their balance restlessly; darting her fingers to the bird's head to fiddle with the dainty leather hood, then finally to remove it. He didn't know many girls like that; within the hour, he was a little in love with her, too. But by then anything to do with the birds was infected with their radiance.

The summer of my tenth year I was sent to stay with my aunt and uncle, and that was the week of my own induction into Jack's world. I loved all houses that were not my own; I loved the routines and rituals of other families, even when those families were, to the casual eye, conventional and dull. Nothing was dull to me. Other people's houses opened to me like enchanted realms simply by virtue of being other and unknown. My cousin Jack's was no exception. It was familiar enough to blunt my shyness, and strange enough to entrance.

There was plenty to be entranced by. My aunt and uncle had money, and lived in the country, on the edge of a Welsh spa town. There were hills visible from the windows, an abundance of hedges and trees around the house, and generally a sense of having left the city far behind for a place where the sound of thrushes and sparrows was louder than the traffic. This, to me, was

Eden; and to wake each morning in a gabled house with more corridors and secret rooms than I had yet had time to count or explore, and look out on a garden the size of a small field, was as much of paradise as I was ever to know.

Jack's bedroom – he was then eighteen – was in a sort of annexe built onto the back of the house. This gave it a rogue feel, as if he were some eccentric offered shelter by a family who asked little of him except that he appear for the evening meal; and this sense of semi-detachment from the rest of the house was wholly appropriate, for the bedroom was like no bedroom I have ever seen.

It was dark, for one thing. The window was a small square, always half-curtained even on a sunny day, and the resulting gloom enhanced the strangeness of the room. It resembled, indeed was, a workshop. The bed was just discernible, a soft, sagging crib with a deep dip in the centre: I got in once, and sank like a badger into its hollow, and felt immediately drowsy. But what dominated the room was the paraphernalia of bird equipment scattered across every surface. There was a table covered with scraps of leather, all in the process of being carved with a strong-bladed, stubby knife. An Anglepoise lamp craned above the jumble of sewing. On an old sideboard stood a set of tiny brass weighing-scales, looking as if they belonged in a doll's house. Next to them, along with various leather straps and ropes, were bundles of small feathers and some miniature brass bells that jingled slightly when shaken, like the sound of a horse's reins. There were several handsome leather gloves with wide flared cuffs that came halfway up the forearm; and a couple of finished bird hoods, exquisite as Spanish leather purses, with sets of tiny strings, feathers and bells.

The room smelt strong. There was something of the young male in it, of course – a definite, peaty odour that was not quite sweat, not quite dirt, but more like the smell of a wild animal's lair. It was tinged with the sharp tang of tanned hide, and with the scent of the strong coffee that my cousin always drank, all day long. When you entered his room, the whole climate was different: you were in Jack country.

He himself treated me with a gentleness and benign neglect that was very different from the bullying attentions of my own brother at home. Jack suffered my silent adoration without impatience or irritation, so preoccupied was he with his own gloomy universe and arcane pursuits that I hardly impinged on his consciousness, except superficially. I hovered, grateful but relaxed, in the suburbs of that universe, observing, absorbing, breathing in with eyes, ears and nose the elements of a world. Jack was unbothered by my quiet, occasionally inquisitive presence. I think my pleasure in discovery of his world pleased him; he was glad to show me everything, to lay it open for my inspection, draw me into the mysteries – of the birds, the hoods, the scales, the bed, the copy of Tolkien dropped on the floor before sleep – that were somehow all connected by a bright thread of magic, and which entered my soul during that week like the light and landscape of a foreign country.

And I was privileged indeed. On the third day of my stay, Jack took me with him when he carried one of his smaller birds, a merlin called Prince, across the fields and farms to the woods a mile away, and flew him. It was a gold-shadowed evening, windless and still, as if the trees and grass and sky had fallen under a spell. The pink and white wild flowers spilling from the hedgerows glowed in the clear but fading day, and only the occasional pigeon or crow flapped between the treetops. I walked, coatless, beside Jack, whose face was serious and alert as he held the tense, hooded bird in his left hand. Every now and again Prince would lose his footing for a moment and shudder his bells, and Jack would duck backwards, away from the raised wings, steadying his hold on the bird's legs with the jess. I was aware of a danger, in the quivering tension of the merlin's body and the fierce clutching of his pronged feet; and in my cousin's body, too, as he concentrated with excitement on keeping the bird calm. There was something strangely poignant about the small, hooded form; blinded, Prince faltered on his master's fist, swaying slightly as he was carried across the dimming fields, like a proud but momentarily disabled man having to surrender to the help of a younger person. I watched with fascination the loose, scaly skin on the legs, and the fearsome talons, like meat hooks; and the infinitely soft feathers on the breast, patterned and overlaid in perfect smoothness across the ribcage that would have fitted into my palm.

The actual flight, I only partly recall. I do know that when we reached the appointed place, I was suddenly invisible, redundant, a rank outsider whose only duty was not to distract either man or bird in the delicate business of the flight, which was more like a ritual between lovers than anything else. I was surplus to requirements, and subsided, to wait and watch.

The lure was taken from the large leather bag Jack had strapped across his body. It was already baited with meat. The merlin's hood was removed, and the ankle cuffs unfastened. My eyes widened in the shadowy blue and gold light. We were in a large field, with tall trees on all sides. Nothing stirred. I smelled the grass, still dewy where it grew long and thick. I was riveted on the bird, which was shifting its weight from foot to foot, and staring with suddenly huge round black eyes. I had never seen such blazing eyes. They seemed to cut right through the air, and every solid object, like lasers. At the same time, they were unseeing: Jack and I were not within the bird's chosen purview. I felt myself tremble slightly. Prince wavered for a second, then raised his wings and suddenly took off with absolute swift sureness, streaking towards the trees.

That is all I remember of the flight. All except the sight of Jack swinging the lure at head height, looking like a shot-putter. The heavy, graceful movement was mesmerising, and went on for some time, since Prince did not seem to want to come out of the trees. There must have been a climactic moment, when the bird swooped in for the 'kill'; but oddly, I remember nothing of it. All I can see, still, is the image of Jack, tall and slender and dark, his face in a rictus of anticipation, hurtling that weighted leather rope in ever-widening circles round his head. He seemed like some bronzed Athenian athlete, standing four-square in the fading golden light, waiting for the moment of ultimate exertion and ultimate triumph.

After that evening, the week tailed off into more prosaic, familiar pleasures and routines. I continued to spend some part of every day in my cousin's cave-like bedroom, assisting his labours, helping to cut pieces for a new glove, and weigh ounces of fresh meat for the hawks, which tore savagely at the shreds of flesh with a precision and intensity that lent hunger a passion I had never before witnessed. But as one day passed into another, and I felt the end of my stay approaching with melancholy inevitability, I sensed also Jack slipping back into the customary solitude of his strange pursuits. He was kind and tolerant towards me yet; but I was a ten-year-old girl, and he was a young man, seemingly unafraid of beaks and talons that could have ripped off his ears and taken out his eyes. He knew the birds would not attack him, of course: I know that now. It was only my own ignorance that feared it.

On my last day, when my parents arrived to collect me, and my aunt cooked a roast beef lunch that we ate on a long table carried out into the back garden, Jack was nowhere to be found. I was sent to see if he was in his bedroom, but he was not there. An empty coffee cup stood on his little deal table, next to the piece of tan leather he had been cutting with the squat knife. The best hood was gone, so was the lure and jess, and the new glove. He hadn't been able to wait any longer before trying it out, I realised. He was out there somewhere now, at this very moment, with Prince trembling on his curled hand, the feel of his claws through the stiff, pungent leather like the clinging of a desperate lover.

THE HAWTHORN TREE

He was crooked like the hawthorn tree, and hardy like the hawthorn tree. It grew at the bottom of his garden in the house where he had been born and where he still lived with his mother. And he loved it. He loved the way it twisted sideways and up, like a lightning fork; the way it leafed out with thousands of the little five-lobed leaves in spring; then the mass of pale-pink blossom in May, so abundant it never failed to astonish him. He loved it in the winter months, too, for then the arthritic stems of the tree were visible; and the black wiry shapes they made were of something struggling under pressure, forcing itself on through suffering and against the odds.

His name was Eric; and he was in charge of a small branch library in a poorer suburb of the city. The other staff, all women, came and went; but he remained. He had been there fifteen years now, and everybody knew him. His manner was gruff, he had no charm, not even of the eccentric kind. Newcomers to the library, customers, took a while to get used to him; but after a while they found they liked to see him there, the same every week, a familiar if peculiar figure in the suburban landscape.

There was nothing wrong with his mind. He had taken a good degree at university, got chartered quicker than most of his peers at the central library where he had begun work, and was now faster than anyone on the computer. But because he was crooked and his sight was near, and he had odd mannerisms and unpolished ways, people often took him for an idiot. He never looked at people straight, and this reinforced the impression of simpleness. But he took most things in all the same.

Of course there were no women. Kids at school had called him 'gay', because they called any misfit boys gay. He had known what it meant, but hadn't minded the word as much as 'spastic'. Not that he had ever challenged any of his persecutors – that had never been his way. What would have been the point? In any battle he was bound to lose.

Except maths. There he outstripped them all, and even won a weird kind of respect from them, because he was so surprisingly good. Some of the girls even came to him for help with their quadratic equations and logarithms. One of them – Suzy Prince, her name was – sat near to him once when he was doing a set of sums for her. He would have done a whole bookful to keep her there, but she sprang up as soon as he handed them back to her, and it never happened again. Most of the time he kept clear of other children, fearing them. He was better on his own.

The library had been his salvation, of course. Who

else would have taken him? He could have run a newsagent's, like his father; but even then his lack of ordinary tact and his unwillingness to pass the time of day in an easy fashion with strangers would have been a handicap. But in the library he was finally accepted, like so many other oddballs who had found sanctuary there. Someone once joked to him that his quirkiness had given him an unfair advantage.

It was early June. The hawthorn was in full bloom, the blossom lying thick as feather boas along the wending branches. Eric glanced up now and again from the kitchen sink where he was scrubbing potatoes for dinner; he could see as far as the river through this back window, but the hawthorn always stopped his gaze before it got that far. His mother shuffled into the room.

'Those kids are in the street again. I hope Mr Bettinson's car is going to be alright.'

The next door neighbour had just bought a new Seat which was now parked, fat and gleaming, among the scratched and faded Maestros and Metros.

'It'll be a red rag to a bull,' said Eric. But he was more worried for himself. One of the boys had once knocked his hat off.

'They need whipping,' said his mother, 'and where are the coppers, I'd like to know.'

She liked to rant a bit; it vented some deeper frustration. Nonetheless, she was right – the teenagers were a hazard. No-one dared challenge them. They owned Jarvis Street like bandits own certain hills.

All through dinner they listened to the boys outside: war-cry whoops went over the rooftops, a football thumped against walls and, once, their front window. Eric hunkered over his pork chop, and ate quickly, as if someone was waiting to take his plate away. Then he made tea for the two of them.

'Are there any more of those biscuits, Eric?'

He found the biscuits and slammed them down on the table.

'Eh, eh, what's up with you? You gave me a fright.'

His mother was used to his moods, which never got more violent than a banged door or the sharp click of a cup in its saucer. Eric did not reply. But later, at bedtime, when the teenagers had finally gone, he said, 'Sorry, Mother.'

The next day was children's story hour in the library. It was advertised with posters depicting clowns, magicians and long-haired princesses. In fact it consisted of three or four melancholy toddlers herded into a corner with Eric, who sat with them on chairs no bigger than chamber pots. He was reading them a story called Polly's Picnic in his special children's voice. They were not listening, and one of the little girls had begun swinging her potty backwards and would any minute crash to the floor; then there would be tears.

'Don't do that,' said Eric, having no effect. 'Sit properly on your chair.'

She ignored him. He read another paragraph. The little girl rocked backwards alarmingly.

'Now stop it!'

Eric had snapped. His voice was hard and sharp. The little girl's face looked stunned, then crumpled in slow motion as the piercing wail went up like a siren.

'Heavens above! What is it now!' rapped Eric. He only did the story hour because the two other staff refused to. They were at the other side of the library, shelving.

It was at that point that the boys came in. Eric didn't see them at first, he was too preoccupied with restoring order in his corner: the little girl, whose momentary hysteria had shrunk to a reproachful expression, was sniffling over a picture book, her thumb to her mouth. By the time Eric looked up, the teenagers were behind the library counter, playing with the computer and the rolls of sticky tape, and smoking cigarettes. A black bird fluttered in Eric's chest.

'Oi!' he shouted from his corner, struggling up from his tiny seat. The biggest of the lads, a boy with long hulking limbs and a small foxy head, turned to look.

He leaned, cool and casual, against the counter and took a long drag on his cigarette, then puffed the smoke into the face of an old lady who had just come through the door and who now hurried out again. The two girl assistants, out of sight, seemed oblivious to the disturbance. Two old gents went on calmly reading their newspapers in the leisure section. Eric scuttled forward.

'Come on now, you can't do that,' he said. He drove

himself forward, hesitating only slightly when he saw the size of the biggest boy's hands.

'Put that cigarette out.'

Eric made a clumsy grab at the boy's fag, as if to snatch it from him.

'I'm *so* frightened . . .' said the boy.

His mate, shrimpish, with a shaved head, was winding the roll of sticky tape round the computer keyboard. A third boy was playing with the electronic scanner, and held it up to Eric's left ear.

'Nope, nothing registers there . . .'

'Right, I'm – I'm calling the police!' said Eric. He dared not touch any of the boys. They would swat him like a fly.

'My uncle's a policeman!' said the boy with the shaved head, spitting the words in Eric's face; which sent them off into fresh waves of laughter.

When Eric got home that night he did not tell his mother about the incident in the library. She would fret, and make another plea for him to find a different kind of job, one where he was not on show, not vulnerable. But there was no such job, and anyway Eric could not think of leaving the library service. He *was* that little library.

Nevertheless he was shaken. The boys had gone of their own accord eventually without his having to tell the police; but they had spun it out, like cats with a mouse, relishing Eric's fear. They had hung about in the lobby for a long time, making a noise and grinding their cigarette butts into the carpet, jeering at him when he told them to leave. If they left off at last it was because they had grown tired of the game, not because he had frightened them.

Eric walked out into the garden after supper. The evening light was still full; it had been a hot, clear day, and the coolness of the late hour was a welcome balm. He shuffled down the flagstoned path past the rose bush and the apple tree, past the place where the cat was buried and the honeysuckle spilled over from next door. He came to the hawthorn tree and put up his hand to the pale blossom. Swifts were screaming overhead, diving through the air like puppet planes. Pure white cloud was strewn across the sky like a casual stroke from an artist's brush. Something rustled in the bushes – a blackbird, perhaps; or one of those small furry creatures that take care never to be seen. Eric looked at the bark on the hawthorn trunk. It was dark, almost black, and deeply ridged, like an ancient, furrowed riverbed. A little ochreous lichen grew here and there in patches like rust. Strange – and strangely comforting – the combination of fresh pink blossom and weathered trunk. Eric held a clutch of flowers once more against his cheek, to be soothed by their softness. Then he ambled back slowly to the house, where his mother was waiting for her tea.

THE WEEKEND BEGINS

There were places to go in town on a Saturday. Teresa and her friends went to them like old men go to the dogs – because that was what you *did*. Anyway, what was there to do at home on a Saturday? And they went because that was what Saturdays meant, that was what gave you that Saturday feeling. It was the one whole day, not clipped at one end by homework, or shadowed at the other by the thought of school tomorrow. It lay waiting, whole as a new unbitten Granny Smith apple. There was even time to get a little bored, in that great double-bed of a day. Time for everything, with time to spare.

But only if you caught it early! Early? There was no such thing as lying in for Teresa and her friends in those days. The streets were quiet when they woke. The cat might stroll into Teresa's little boxroom and alight softly, like a seagull on a sand dune, on her bed; her father might arrive a little later than usual with the cup of sweet red tea, and it might stay there next to her bed a little longer, until a creamy orange disc had begun to pucker the surface. But the morning was old by nine o'clock all the same. In sunny weather the first children were already out playing in the streets, and the baker five minutes' walk away had long rattled up his shutters.

For Saturday was shops, too: a dark, ragged line of them set back from the noisy road, next to the aerodrome of the cinema, and opposite the Bluebell Inn. Like a string of hutches, they were; large hutches, too large for the owners to fill with goods half the time – and each with its own smell. The only proper shop, stacked tightly and neatly with wares, was the hardware and electrical – and for that reason it held no charm. But Lacey's the newsagent's – ah! Lacey's was dirty; there was dust on the floor and flies in the window on old yellowed Beanos; there was always the same ancient box of Black Magic with a faded pink rosebud on the front. A fat white cat slept in a small patch of sun in the window, between the plastic pencil-cases and the bleached exercise books priced in wavery writing; and the shop was filled with a smell wholly unidentifiable but wholly recognisable and comforting, consisting perhaps of old custard creams, damp newspapers, cat hairs, matchboxes, dried-up liquorice sticks, banana toffee, and Mr Lacey's hair oil. But all these things were like hawthorn and foxgloves on a walk in the country – they were what you expected; and when Teresa walked into that shop to dawdle among the comics while her mother paid the paper bill and bought cigarettes, she breathed in the scents of tobacco and chocolate, of slim packets of butterscotch, lemon bonbons piled dustily in jars, and the mystery of the grown-up boxes of Terry's All Gold balanced on high shelves behind Mr Lacey's head as he served.

But this was only shopping! Saturdays were for shopping when there was nothing else on, or friends were on holiday. Proper Saturday mornings were for the indoor market, or for the Empire Pool, or later, for the flicks. So now Teresa and her friends Katriona and Christine are waiting at the bus stop, dressed in their best flared trousers, though still with the same old anoraks on top. They have their money ready in their hands. They have their little flat purses decorated with coloured beads. They have hair clips of peeling nickel holding back their greasy hair – greasy because Saturday night is bath night – and in their pockets are tubes of sweets like bank-rolls of pennies. Always sweets. Refreshers and Ice Breakers, Liquorice Pinwheels, Sherbert Fountains and Aniseed Jellies, Flying Saucers and Blackjacks.

And the bus comes rocking and careering and lurching to a stop; and it's up on the back platform and straight upstairs. A quick glance confirms – yes! The front seats are free! Nobody else up here but two old ladies in headscarves and a young man with a disconsolate fag between finger and thumb.

Are they being naughty? Will they be found out? There's the clump, clump, steady, of the conductor's boots on the steep steps, and he swings towards them, all the while looking from the window, hardly noticing them at all. But they still fear that any minute they'll be found to be too young, too small, wrongly dressed, or guilty of sucking their sweets before they've had lunch. But no – they've got away with it again. The conductor's machine is sticking out its tongues of smooth blue tickets, one of sixpence, one of three, another of tuppence. And the rummaging in the chestnut leather bag for change, the lovely rustle of invisible coins, and the threepenny bits produced, one for each of them, tarnished and smelling of fillings.

In town it's straight to the market – no detours, for there are only two or three places marked on their map as yet – and up the wide, shallow staircase to the galleries, where the strange and curious stalls are: the second-hand records, the model-railway man, a hardware place selling fuses and light bulbs out of their packets. And the pet shops. This is what Teresa and her cronies have come for. Not to buy – oh no! But to look. Just to look. For there, beyond the weird rough cafe that always has the same three purple-faced people sitting in its open pews, is the pile of hutches and cages, heaped like a Moroccan bazaar. Cages, did I say? Yes – and empty cages by the look of it! Not a creature in sight, not a pair of bright eyes or a tuft of fur. But come closer, and if you crouch close to the bars, and let your eyes get accustomed to the gloom and camouflage of straw and sawdust, you might make out the humped back of a sleeping rabbit, the tail of a snoozing kitten, the ears of a hamster delicate as half-opened petals on a cyclamen.

And it is enough, this crouching next to the cages of

slumbering rodents and snake-heaps of kittens, trying to disentangle with your eyes one from another, to see which head goes with which tail. There is a warm, pungent smell – rather delicious to the noses of the young girls, like the smell of a horse's neck. There is the echoing cacophony of cheeps and chirps going up to the glass roof and resounding there, mixing with the cries of the fruit sellers below. And the girls' faces, rosy as apples, as they gaze into the big cage with the new puppy that still seems a little squashed and not quite set into his final shape, so recently was he pushed out into the light from his mother's belly.

The pet-stall woman tolerates them for a while, then moves them on with an 'Anything I can get you, girls?' and a look far harder than anything they get at home. The woman is huge and brawny, with hair like oiled black string and hands all speckled with the ochre grit of dog biscuits. She drinks from a pint mug of tea, and talks all the time to a skinny young lad with sad eyes. Teresa and her friends rise reluctantly from the cages and drift away, clutching and touching each other for safety and for fun in the squalor and bustle and danger of the market.

What will they do now? Buy Chelsea buns, of course, and tear off bits inside the bag, eating them as they walk. The dough is fresh and soft, and there are specks of spice among the currants. And the best bit: a sticky, sugared crust that can be unwound from its spiral like a necklace.

And it is still not eleven o'clock. Teresa looks up at the big square clock-face in the middle of the market and sees with a little thrill the hand actually moving, stiffly, to the next minute mark. They pass the jewellery stall, and the handbag stall, and the place where her mother buys material to make dresses. (The man there is quite different from the rest – he has waved white hair like a woman, and a fancy gold watch.) And it is not yet eleven o'clock. It is still the beginning of Saturday; they are still picking at the edges of it, and of their buns, seeing how long they can make it last before they reach the soft fragrant centre and devour it in two blissful bites.

APPLE TART

I came down from my room that day only when the moment could not be put off any longer. We had guests. It was a Sunday in July and very hot; and my mother had ordered the table to be carried out into the garden so we could have lunch with the ladybirds and wasps.

I felt a pang when I saw the long table laid with a brilliant white cloth. It reminded me of an Italian wedding; or more likely, a scene from my own childhood, when we had regularly eaten outside on summer Sundays, and the cats had pranced around us on the lawn, making dashes at the long cloth before collapsing in the sun as if someone had pulled a string in their legs.

My uncles and aunts were coming today. I had not seen them for over a year, since before this thing started. The last ten months were elongated in my mind, for in that time I had become a different person; and the daily application of so much will power had not made the weeks go faster. At fifteen, I had brought myself under control, and I had done it alone. I was proud of my achievement, but it had come at a cost.

The trouble was, the others did not understand this, and so a great deal of secrecy was necessary.

When I came down from my room, I could not help but be cheered by the sun. I was wearing my usual layers – even in the summer I was cold – but it was like stepping into a warm bath, entering that garden after the chilly dimness of the house. The light made the skin on my hands and wrists bloodless, the colour of dirty snow; the fingertips were still bluish. But I might have been any normal person, joining her family for a celebration on a sunny day: that was the thought that sparked inside me as I crossed the long lawn. I had my flashes of sanity.

The first thing that happened was that my Auntie Julia did not recognise me. There was a polite, embarrassed silence when I greeted everybody, then Uncle Norman leant forward and pressed my hand, and said,

'You're looking lovely, Sarah.'

My Auntie Julia, a large and large-hearted woman, looked at me for a moment from behind the glinting panes of her glasses. Then it came.

'It's not Sarah!'

She looked around her, appealing for contradiction, genuinely amazed at my transformation.

'But you used to be –'

I was used to such reactions.

'But you've gone to nothing!'

She looked up at my mother, who was cutting up bread, beautiful milky-white French bread with a thin golden crust, and handing round little saucers of unsalted butter. My mother gave her a small, troubled smile.

'Hasn't she, Norman? She's a tiny slip of a thing! And she used to be so –'

I winced under the spotlight that had been turned on me. Suddenly I was aware that I was the only one at the table wearing three layers of clothes. Still I shuddered when a breeze passed over. I filled my glass with water. There was no way Auntie Julia was going to let the subject go, so I responded at last.

'I used to weigh ten and a half stone, Auntie Julia,' I announced with satisfaction. I reached forward for my glass, and my eyes fell for the hundredth time on the slender fragility of my wrist. That wrist was my achievement.

'You were a bonny girl,' said Auntie Julia, unmollified. It angered me when people failed to understand that being fat makes you miserable.

'And now look at you!'

'Julia –' Her husband cut in. Like the rest of my family, he was a sensitive and diplomatic man. He changed the subject, and soon the talk had turned to my cousin Jeremy and his escapades in the world of acting. Thank God for colourful cousins. Now I could get through the hour in peace.

A wasp landed on my white china plate and I studied its intricate patterns as it crawled from one white surface to another. How slender insects are, I thought;

you never see an overweight wasp. It is only humans who destroy the lineaments of beauty by wadding their bones with blubber. But people seemed to have forgotten this. There was a conspiracy to pretend that it was normal and good to be a little overweight. And so they punished and nagged anyone who dared to disagree, and who reproached them by being sleek and unspoiled. I was prepared for this; I had got used to being different and therefore feared in the last year. People accused me of losing my sense of humour: all the usual tactics for pressurising the brave loner into conformity, so that her discipline and truth shall not disturb and annoy.

'Butter, Sarah?' My Uncle Bruce innocently proffered the lump of fat.

'Oh, no thanks.' I ducked backwards as if he had been holding a dish of sheep's eyes. I picked up my disc of bread and began my usual strategy of picking tiny crumbs off the crust, and eating them slowly, one by one. Occasions such as this demanded all my ingenuity, but I had had a great deal of practice.

I watched my parents handing round the gleaming serving dishes. It was like a scene from a French impressionist painting. And I thought: this is just the sort of thing I loved in the old days. Then, I would have drunk without stint, as well as eating a great deal of everything my mother had cooked, without hesitation or constraint. I would have sipped diluted beer and sugar before lunch, or even had a full goblet of red wine with my meal, and felt the heady liquor warming my veins and mingling with the sun, the talk, and the delicious flavours of roast lamb and runner beans. My past. How much I had had to give up! What a rich palette I had sacrificed for my austerely monochrome life. What secrets I had had to keep, and how lonely my task had been. I doubted if any one of the people around me had the faintest idea of what I had put myself through for my achievement. And they would not find out.

So when the beans and carrots came round, I heaped my plate. I made a show of asking for the pepper. I even pretended to take a little gravy (I could always leave it, along with the roast potato that smelt so enticing I would have considered, in a reckless moment, putting on half a pound in order to eat it); and of course I kept my glass of water topped up. Conversation was my great ally. I had never, until recently, been one to talk much at the dinner table; but on days such as this, it was absolutely necessary. There is only so much fiddling you can do with your food before you actually have to lift a forkful to your mouth.

And I did enjoy the look, and the smell, of the food. I was a connoisseur of scents, and extracted from them an intense pleasure. The smell of the roast meat as it curled forwards from my father's knife; of the buttered peas as they were handed round in their scalloped dish; of the gravy as it was spooned over little heaps of translucent beans, and mashed into hot, crisp potatoes;

these things were a delicious torment to me. But they were also luxuries I allowed myself, because they held no consequences, no anguish, so long as I simply watched others consuming them. I spun out the eating of my plain vegetables as long as possible meanwhile, and congratulated myself on being able to make of such austere fare a feast. For every meal was a religious rite for me now: my day was centred on food as a Christian's life is centred on God.

Blasphemy? Perhaps. But I lived a blasphemous life. I spurned the good fruits of the earth, and worshipped the idol of my own diminishing mirror image. Never underestimate the selfishness of obsession. My world was narrow and private as a madman's. Did I say mad? I think even then, in the middle of it, somewhere in myself I knew.

My Auntie Julia kept giving me looks throughout the meal. She was not appeased, she was not going to be so easily reconciled to my new, fleshless form. I eyed, with contemptuous fascination, her overloaded plate, and the great piled forkfuls of food that disappeared into her stretched mouth. It was incomprehensible to me that anyone could eat such a meal and not be in despair for days afterwards.

And the meal went on, unbelievably. The sun beat down on our heads, a warm breeze lifted the corners of the tablecloth, the wasps continued to hover magnetically above our glasses, a ladybird inched across my lap, and the soft clash of china and glass was absorbed by the lustrous hedges and the carpet of grass. My mother had picked four flame-coloured roses and put them in a glass in the middle of the table; their liquorous scent came to me in cool gusts periodically.

And Auntie Julia watched. Busily, I delved into my heap of greens, feigning relish and greedy appetite. Heartily I laughed and joined in the talk, and even asked for more carrots. And all the while Auntie Julia's eyes, not yet recovered from the first shock of seeing me, kept their vigil on my plate, on my fragile wrists, on my covered neck and shoulders.

It was when my mother appeared from the house, bearing a tray of apple pie and cream, that something broke in me and dissolved. Was it the sunlight, the conspiracy of aunts and uncles, of green grass and white cloth, of wine and cut glass; the drowse of contentment that was settling over our party like a gauzy web as people rolled up their shirt sleeves and loosened their shoes under the table, stretching their legs and asking for their glasses to be recharged? My father refilled his pipe; my Auntie Gwen undid the top button of her blouse; the conversation turned to old memories: of my parents' wedding, of shared holidays, of the time my sister and I got locked in the outhouse.

'You were a funny little thing,' said Uncle Norman, smiling at me with memories in his eyes. Auntie Julia regarded me, watchfully. I was looking at my mother, who was sinking a knife into the deep breast of the apple tart. A breath of fragrant steam escaped. I saw the hot juices run as she lifted high wedges onto clean white plates. The cream was thick and yellow, in a blue jug.

'You were always a pretty little thing, and always up to something secret,' he said again, back deep in the past now. It was true – I had been a slender child, before I got fat in my early teens. Now I was my old self again: a bird-light girl, with sparrow bones.

I stared down at the triangle of pie set before me. I so wanted to eat it; why couldn't I eat it? I could smell the tangy syrup, I could almost taste the flaking buttery crust. Why couldn't I eat it? I longed not only for the taste of the apple pie in my mouth, but for all that lost innocence, that past, when I had been a little girl who ate what was put in front of her, without fear or pretence, without anxiety or disguise. Back then, I had eaten my apple pie, with cream, and then got down from the table and played on the grass, the meal quite forgotten. I had teased the cat and rolled on my back and looked up at the sky through the cracks of my fingers, making the light flash and sparkle. My body was nothing to me but lightness and energy. I took it for granted as I took for granted the trees and flowers; and the food, as good and natural as the summer sun.

And watching my mother then, as she lifted the spoon to her mouth and enjoyed her apple pie and cream, so utterly unselfconscious and guiltless, I felt tears prick the backs of my eyes. Normality; blessed normality.

'Aren't you eating your tart?' My Auntie Julia smiled at me with quizzical encouragement. I would have to pretend to, in order to put her off the scent.

'Of course!' I replied, raising my spoon in exaggerated relish, ready to dive in. But I could not see what was in front of me, for my eyes were completely veiled with tears.

A MATTER OF IMPORTANCE

On the way to his three o'clock Friday lecture on Satire in the Age of Johnson, Professor Felps passed his younger colleague, Kurt Weiss, in the corridor. The new lecturer greeted his senior with bashful warmth. He was, after all, the author of *Byron's Last Stand*, now in its fourth edition. Felps wore a radiant, beatific smile, the smile of a man communing with long-dead greatness. Herr Weiss was left feeling rays of light had picked him out for a moment; but it was light from some cold, mineral planet that had momentarily strayed into the wrong universe.

For his part, Professor Felps noticed only one more apparition among others: a kindly, blushing apparition, more reverent than most. Wasn't that the young man he had conversed with in German at the start-of-term shindig? Eager chap, full of high ideals. There was no doubt about it, these Europeans were better trained, had higher standards, could be relied on to have read their Spenser and Milton, putting most of his young home-grown colleagues to shame.

Felps had something of Regency air. Was it the amateur actor in him? Certainly the stage training helped. His days with the Little Morton Players had increased his 'presence' – that ineffable quality that stilled a roomful of restless students as soon as he walked through the door. But mostly it was his own property and creation, this aura of dandified nonchalance and confidence he gave off, so that he would not have looked at all anomalous in a wig of rambling curls and a pair of tight scarlet hose with emerald gaiters. The drab uniform of twentieth-century Everyman was incongruous on his sprightly form; only his head of thickly-waved hair, brushed forward like the upswept locks of a Roman emperor, showed him in his true colours. And his eyes, of course – round and staring as the eyes of a rapt clairvoyant, as if he were perpetually playing Ariel, and overdoing it.

Arriving at the door to the lecture theatre, Professor Felps paused dramatically before entering. Then, composed, he swept in. He did not look up, but took the podium immediately and decisively, like a man taking charge of the deck of a ship. Then, after a few hushed moments, during which his audience adjusted to the sudden authority in their midst, he raised his ready face, addressing, as he had been taught, a spot in the far left-hand corner of the ceiling, and with mock-ingratiation, embarked on the career of Richard Burbage.

The students – middle years, at the end of their first semester, but still malleable – gave him no trouble. Not that he would have noticed if they did: it was not for him to notice the students, after all. As Professor Felps saw it, his task was to give of his enchanting self for exactly fifty minutes, in a certain place at a certain hour, several times a week; to disperse his magical influence like angel dust over those lucky or enlightened enough to lay themselves open to it. Whether there were three startled faces or thirty-three bored ones was not his concern, and had no effect on his performance. For make no mistake: it was a performance. Let those who stayed away live to regret their lost chances.

He was quite lost in his own eloquence now. The brutal, low-ceilinged room, designed by philistines, and starkly functional as a laboratory, was transformed by his magnificence to a spotlit corner of the Garrick stage, where powdered nymphets trembled in the wings. Felps heard his voice soaring to the polystyrene tiles, then dropping to a stage whisper, gathering his listeners in. His eyes became even more rounded with trance-like wonder; his arms were flung out in gestures of abandon. He paced here; he paced there; he returned to the stock, stupid column of the lectern that so spoiled his command of the stage, but which he subdued with a gentle clasp of both hands, as he delivered his final lines with just the right dying fall, before lifting up his eyes one last time to the heavens, and thanking his students humbly for their patient appreciation.

There, it was done. A palpable sigh of relaxation loosened the room, as if a great corset had been unlaced. A polite shuffling of papers and gathering of coats declared the shift from one mode to another: suddenly the students were junior clerks again, resuming their group identity, released from the lecturer's spell. Their real business – the exchange of prosaic information on essay deadlines, and gossip about housemates – could now be continued uninterrupted. They suddenly filled the room, and Professor Felps was a lone, gratuitous presence on the platform, a man in need of an exit stage-left, with no alternative but the ignominious retreat, mingling with the audience as he departed, smiling distantly, from the room.

It was his great concession to the department, the Friday lecture. He had been asked to do more. But since the preferment, he had settled with himself the exact quantity of undergraduate teaching he was prepared to undertake, and nothing further. The three o'clock Friday slot was in itself enough of a humiliation. Everyone knew that only the keenest students would attend at this twilight hour already infected with a holiday feel, so that those industrious enough to turn up did so with the consciousness of their own benevolence, indulging the lecturer in his whimsical desire to distract them for a few remaining moments before they were released into the bacchanal of the weekend.

So, it was Professor Felps's gift, his generous boon to the department, and to the students, of his good offices, which they hardly deserved. For had he not been passed over in the appointment of a new Head of English only two years previously? Having temporarily stepped into that very post, at the convenience of the department (and no little inconvenience to himself), had he not then been set aside in favour of – well, we all know to whom the position had gone, finally. Enough said. But Professor Felps – wounded, diminished – had stayed on, with nothing but a strip of tape on his door, stuck there as a memorial to his brief reign as actor-manager of the whole caboodle, bearing the inscription: Professor Duncan Felps, Head of Department. It was, it seemed, impossible to remove. The glue was fiendishly strong. There was some confusion among the students as a result, for they were sure they had been told that – – –, who shall remain nameless, was in fact the Head. Surely there was some mistake somewhere?

Felps stayed on. It was a gracious act, the act of a nobleman resigned to going unrecognised among the *hoi polloi*. A man must earn his crust, after all; must live among his fellow men for at least part of his time on earth. Render unto Caesar, et cetera. Thus it was that Professor Felps consented to give three lectures a week for one semester of each academic year; the other semester, and the vacations (getting shorter!) generally being spent on secondment to other, more important institutions, or in writing his mildly distinguished books on The Age of Satire, and The Decline of Prosody.

And how did the Professor cope with his anomalous status in the English Department? It was not one of the better universities, after all. At Oxford he would have been happy to accept his place as one among many, for there he would have been a lion among lions. But here? They were lucky that he chose to grace their corridors at all; they were infinitely fortunate to enjoy his three o'clock Friday lecture. He cast his pearls before swine only as often as he could bear; but he did it with conviction, for his own self respect.

And now there was this business with the marking. Jenkins was behind it, of course; couldn't resist wielding the sceptre now and then, just to keep him in his place. Anyone would think *he* was Head of Department. But really – two lots of second-year scripts on Don Juan! When he was just sinking his teeth into the third chapter of his new book on Addison and Steele. These people had no conception of the needs of real academics – the ones like himself, who actually wrote books.

As Felps reached his own cubicle – it was hardly a *room* – and flung open the door with a flourish, he saw with horror that someone had actually entered the room in his absence and left three sturdy piles of student scripts on his desk. Rank cowardice! Whoever had done it had not had the nerve to face him. Apart from the scandal of breaking into his private room, there was the number of essays – easily twice as many as he had anticipated. Student numbers had risen sharply in the last few years, of course – roughly in inverse proportion to the quality of the work they produced.

Who handed him essays on Goethe written in German now? Which of them bothered to read the whole of *The Faerie Queene*, or got past the first five hundred pages of *Clarissa*? And yet they gaily churned out reams of vapid twitterings for his exquisite mind to ponder. Who, in this godforsaken centre of mediocrity, actually recognised Duncan Felps for what he was?

The eyes were not tranced in wonderment now. They were stretched still in that strange, fixed expression that was half smile, half will-o'-the-wisp, but a shaft of steel had hardened them. Professor Felps, lifting with scorn the coversheet on the first pile of essays, as if it were a note from the *sans culottes* informing him of his imminent execution, considered how he should react to this latest insult. Was it even worth confronting Jenkins? Wasn't it beneath his dignity to respond? He disliked anything ugly. On the other hand, the prospect of a brief, pungent exchange with that officious little memo-writer . . . well, it was tempting. But he was not ready to resign. And one must always be willing to resign once embarked on a scene of that kind.

Then he remembered Kurt Weiss. Yes! Dr Weiss, so anxious to be of service, would pick up the slack. He was, after all, still in his probationary year. To relieve Professor Felps of some of his labours would be a pleasure to the younger man: a privilege, in fact.

It was not Weiss's specialism, of course. There was that. He was a Renaissance man. But what of it? That was half the trouble with the new generation of academics – they were far too narrow, too locked into one mean little groove. It would do the German good to have to mark fifty essays on Byron; loosen up some of that Teutonic stuffing and starch. One had to learn somehow – in at the deep end was often best. Why, when he had been starting out . . .

He got on the blower. To the secretary, naturally, not to Weiss himself. There was a charming young girl – reminded him of Caroline Lamb – who was most obliging. She would sort it out, get things shifted round a bit. No need to get Jenkins involved. It was a small detail, after all; an almost insignificant rearrangement that no-one sensible could possibly object to. So it could be kept between the three of them. Authorisation? Oh, but Felps had once been Head of Department, didn't she know?

So it was that the young, blushing Dr Weiss received a hefty parcel of extra manuscripts to mark that same afternoon, just ten minutes after Professor Felps had left the building, sauntering mildly through the soulless labyrinth of corridors like an innocent abroad, as if he hardly belonged to the place. And as the Professor stepped with a sprightly foot into his car, Dr Weiss focussed with surprise, then confusion, then with growing agitation on the wodge of papers dumped with such horrible finality on his desk by the secretary. On top was a loose sheet of A4, informing him that the papers were 'unforeseen surplus', at the decree of the Department.

To whom was he to appeal? Byron was completely beyond his competence. It was outside his remit – surely Jenkins knew that? Wasn't Professor Felps the Byron man? Surely there had been some mistake.

And yet he was reluctant to object. It would look so bad, especially in his very first semester. No, in fact the more he thought about it, he could hardly blot his copy book with such petty complaints at this delicate stage of his career. He wanted to get on. And Professor Felps – well, it would be a privilege to mark his course. So what if he had to spend the whole weekend reading Don Juan.

A week later, the fifty scripts (of a rather poor standard on the whole, the German thought) were delivered in three neatly squared-off, string-tied piles, back to the secretary's office. Who was the second marker, Dr Weiss wished to know. Second marker? Oh, let me just see. Yes, that would be Professor Jenkins this year. He occasionally helped out with the Romantics. Professor Felps? Oh no! Professor Felps had completed all the marking he was obliged to do, and gone on holiday for a week to Scotland. No, he could not be reached.

When, returning from the Highlands, Professor Felps found a letter in a sealed envelope placed prominently on his desk, he assumed it must be an invitation to give a paper at one of the postgraduate seminars he had seen advertised on the Department noticeboards. Opening it with his usual briskness, he was mildly surprised to find it was from that impertinent fool, Jenkins, summoning him – summoning! – to his office at 2.15 that afternoon.

What nerve. Felps considered whether or not to go. It couldn't be anything really important; he hadn't committed any misdemeanours. There was that business over the Byron scripts . . . but Jenkins wouldn't have been involved there. The second marker was young Merryweather, wasn't it? So it must be some laughable flexing of his muscles: an attempt to ruffle Felps's feathers for the fun of it.

Well, two could play at that. He'd keep Jenkins waiting. What a cheek! Didn't he know who Felps was? Good God, if necessary he'd threaten to – wouldn't he? But he hadn't even done anything! No, he'd let him stew. The man's impudence was unbelievable. Hadn't he seen the sign on Felps's door? Didn't he know who he was dealing with?

PEACE

The divorced lawyer sat alone in his large, well-ordered living room in which very little living now went on. He was staring without looking at his high wall of books, with their cracked spines and covers thinned and supple. Next to them his music collection hung like an archive of his past: the Bach cello sonatas now sacred with melancholy; the racks of Bob Dylan, Joan Baez, Joni Mitchell, all promising instant time travel and a painful-sweet, sudden flaring of forgotten modes of feeling.

These were what he was left with now, the extensions of himself, the last things to which he was fixed. There were other objects, too, of course: things that vibrated weirdly with their continued existence through all the changes of his adult life; certain cups and cutlery, for instance, that had accompanied him on each journey to a new staging post. That a cup with a primrose painted clumsily on it should survive those upheavals and still sit on his kitchen shelf, while human beings had been discarded, was mysterious. His possessions were painful to him for this reason; but for this reason also he cherished them.

It was not often that he sat in this way, with no visible occupation. The truth was that he feared it. The air contained pressures that it had not contained when his family lived here with him. Lived here with him! That phrase was not right: it suggested they were only staying, and might go. That was part of the new way of talking that he used now. But he would not have used it in his old life. Then there was no question of their not living here; the very idea would have seemed obscene or mad.

The pressures began to throng around him now, the weight of emptiness in the room. With a quick movement he reached out for a paperweight that lay on the low table in front of him. It was a beautiful object, extremely heavy, solid and smooth. It was formed from some kind of blue glass into a crustacean-like shape that squatted in the hand with a surprising gravity. But the loveliest thing about it was its strange dispersal of colour: the pigment seemed absolutely sheer, and yet was not transparent. It had the purity of an early summer sky of pale turquoise, the kind of sky that hangs like an immense veil of perfect gauze, without blot or variation, to the very edges of vision.

He turned his hands round the paperweight as if he were warming them on it, though the glass was cool. He did this almost unconsciously, his eyes meanwhile fixed on some inward thought, as a child rubs a satin-bordered blanket across its lips. His eyes were the same hot-cool colour as the glass, a vivid flamey blue that was the more striking now that his face had faded from its first rich colouring. He sat in the silent room, a slim figure with cornflower eyes, his small brown hands slowly turning the little boulder of blue glass.

His eyes came to rest on a photograph of his wife and child, and he put the paperweight down. Then he got up and pulled the curtains shut with a brisk movement. He switched on the radio and got the shipping forecast, then a bit of Stockhausen. He turned off the radio and put the TV on, wanting the presence of some personality to commandeer the room. He settled on a repeat of *Dad's Army* and was relieved to be instantly taken over by Captain Mainwaring's unshakeable rotundity and gentle bullying. He sat and watched with a half-smile of wonder and delight as the familiar characters went through their unvarying routines like players in a children's pantomime. He knew these men! The way Sergeant Wilson wore his glengarry at a languid droop; and young Frank held his rifle like a bicycle pump; and the doddering Godfrey, dressed like a rag doll in his sagging khakis, stammering his objections to some over-exciting scheme.

The man sat watching these ageless figures as they folded up three decades into a small and insignificant concertina. They had not changed or moved forward. And suddenly, it seemed to him, neither had he. For nothing in between had superseded this bunch of characters in their power to affect him. His wife, his daughter even, were realisations of what these men had prefigured. His love for them had been rehearsed in his love for these caricatures and oddballs, with their trademark habits and phrases. When the programme came to an end, he leaned forward to turn the signature music up, and the strains of a quavering voice billowed through the room like some unquenchable proof of continuity.

But then there was silence again. The man listened to it for a moment and felt the temptation to give in to it. His hands stiffened on his legs and he was unable to move head or limbs. It might be stronger than he was – in which case, why fight it? Let the silence embalm him like an insect. Let it make him finally still.

He was tired after all of running from it. Each day for the last year and a half he had had to summon reserves of energy to avoid the silence. He had dodged it like a swamp, skirting it or quickly hopping across it on stepping stones. He had tried to drown it out, tried leaving it behind, tried overwhelming it with visits fom noisy friends. At the end of the evening it still awaited him, endlessly patient. It defeated his resources and did not get weaker with time.

Usually he did not give room to these thoughts for long. He decided to sweep them out now. And he saw himself rising from the chair, rising quickly in one smooth easy movement. But it didn't happen. He was fixed, immobile; and the more he did not move, the less it seemed he would be able to. The empty room pressed on his shoulders, his knees, his hands, his face, even. Only his eyes moved, travelling over the cold fireplace with its starched bouquet of dried grasses, the mantelpiece pointlessly propping photos of those that were gone, the high wall of books in alphabetical order.

But he had the room exactly as he wanted it. It expressed him absolutely. He had had a new floor laid now that he was childless again, and the polished wood blocks glowed with a dark lustre that gave him great pleasure. He had been very anxious to lay the new floor quickly, as if he were cementing over dead bodies.

The room was really perfect, a work of art in its way, with its spare white furniture and white walls, and clean wooden surfaces. Light filled it in the daytime like a clean white empty bowl. It was a room that, by its spartan purity, created its own silence. Sounds, smell and clutter affronted it like pollution.

And now, in the evening, he felt himself shrinking under the whiteness of the walls and the relentless silence. Of course he knew there was no going back. He had chosen this solitude, had craved to be free of the bonds that had pressed on him as tightly as the silence now did. Trapped! The very word was like a physical pang that bit into his flesh. He had been a caught animal, a fox with its leg in a snare, gnawing at the leg that he might escape, mutilated but free. He knew it would be a mutilation, that he was escaping from one pain into another. So how could he now complain?

He had things to do before morning. He hung onto

this thought as if it were very important. Then with an abrupt, almost violent movement, he sprang up from his chair and walked out of the French doors and into the garden.

It was one of those still summer evenings that take a long time to die. He walked past the long daisies that were almost closed, the yellow rose bush and a flaring clump of red-hot pokers. There was a draught of expensive perfume from the roses, and he trailed his hand over the cool, firm polyps of the pokers. Patches of aubretia and mallow showed like crowds of small faces in the near-dark. There was a sense of presences, more so than in the daytime, and he was taken aback for a moment by the large stars of a white clematis climbing the trellis above the rockery. He walked slowly on soft, stealthy feet the length of the narrow garden, his limbs unfolded and light now. Out here was a different silence, containing the breath of the trees and flowers, and the shy congregation of the stars. He reached the end of the garden where there was a great sycamore, and entered the deeper shadow of the tree with a little thrill of fear, so dense and mysterious was it in the darkness.

He remembered there was a cat buried under the tree. Suddenly this scene from his other life blew in on him like a powerful odour, and he closed his eyes and reeled a little. Amanda, his little girl, had been very solemn and graceful with the poor stiffened lump of the cat's body, insisting on placing it in the little grave herself. He saw her as she knelt down under the tree, holding out the cat as if it were a sacrifice to the gods, her face oddly reverent and grown-up. She whispered as she lay the animal down: there, there, Gypsy, now you'll go to heaven.

He came to, and strode back up the path, brushing the overspill of fuchsia roughly as he passed. Back in the house he went round switching off lights and locking doors, doing his last few tasks before bed. He had reverted to his old routines, and now adhered to them more rigidly than ever. Passing through the hall he caught his face in the big mirror and paused for a moment, noticing that his eyes were staring rather wildly. His hair was standing up at one side and in the bleaching light of the hall he could see very clearly the skull beneath his features. There, unmistakably, were the species marks: the deepening pits of the eyes, quite visible, and the cheek and jaw bones prominent. He bared his teeth and realised he was a living skeleton. His eyes looked out, trapped, like strangers in a face that seemed to be going about its own business of decay. He was being hurried towards death. He was forty-two.

Climbing the stairs, he felt a kind of peace at last, having completed his evening's quota of suffering. He could be let off now until the next night. Gratefully, he registered a sudden drop into tiredness; and as he pulled back the covers on the old double bed that had seen so much intimate history, he thought this is what death must be like: the limp, relieved stepping into the smooth, cool sheets of the shroud; and then lying still and alone in the darkness, listening to the beats of the clock

THE FOUNDLING

He retraced his steps for a few yards. He was returning from his nightly walk, and just as he passed the big Victorian villa in the block before his own, he heard a bleating, a thin steel pin of a sound, so tiny he could easily have missed it.

He walked back, listening; there was nothing. Then from the hedge, a small rustling. He stopped, alert, and waited, and looked with big eyes into the darkness. Then came the tiny bleating again, very near this time. It was a kitten. It must have strayed somehow from the house. He could not quite make it out yet, in the darkness. But there was a movement, quite close to him, in the bottom of the laurels. He crouched down to try and get a better view, making no abrupt movements that might frighten off the creature. The moon shone down cold on the grass, and the air nipped.

When the little bundle of dark fur eventually put out a tentative paw and walked out into the moonlight, he rejoiced. The kitten seemed to trust him. It was presenting itself – wasn't it? There was an appeal in its round, glossy eyes. Well, it must belong to the people in the house. He would just return it to its owners, and then all would be well. It was rather late by now, of course.

The kitten stood there, mewing vigorously in the moonlight. Its whole body contracted in the mewing. The man could see how young it was, barely weaned, with its face still hardly emerged from the soft halo of black fur, and the little legs still stumpy. Its tail was a fluffy triangle, all its downy black hairs standing out as if electrified. The kitten did not look at the man or rub his hand. It was too primitive as yet. It just stood there helplessly bleating in the chilly air, waiting for it knew not what.

Well, he must rescue it. He couldn't possibly leave it. It seemed to have chosen him. Yes – lucky, really, that he had heard the little thing crying out in the darkness, and gone back.

There was a light on in the house. So despite the hour – it was past eleven – he rang the bell. Then he waited, the kitten making delicious squirmy movements against his chest, clinging to his jumper with its tiny claws. Under his hand it felt so small and fragile, like a mouse. And yet strong, too, clinging on for dear life.

A man came to the door, frowning suspicously. He was in his dressing gown and his hair stuck up at the back. No, it was not their kitten. Perhaps he knew whose . . . ? No, sorry. Now, if you'd excuse me . . . The door clunked softly shut. The kitten gave a pin-prick bleat.

The other houses were dark and unavailable, sunk in

sleep. The man shrank from approaching them. The kitten had worked its way up onto the promontory of his shoulder and was wobbling there, its fur tickling his ear. He put up a hand, and felt the butterfly heart and miniature ribcage under his palm. Perhaps the little fellow was hungry? He took him back to his own house.

'It's only for tonight. I'm giving you back in the morning!'

He lectured the kitten while watching as it drank milk from a saucer, lapping up the liquid rather clumsily, not yet expert. He mashed up some tinned sardines: the kitten sniffed gingerly at the edges, then nibbled daintily, his flat, button eyes closing in pleasure.

The purring was prodigious. Man and cat sat in the living room in the winged armchair, the heat from the gas fire tingling and flushing the man's face, and radiating through the kitten's tiny frame. The purring began abruptly, loudly. It seemed absurd that such a noise should come from something so small.

He was quite a houseproud person. The rooms were sparely but elegantly furnished with choice pieces he had picked up in antique shops and warehouses. The floor was sanded and polished and scattered with beautiful old Wolsey rugs in faded shades of duck-egg blue and rose. The coverings on the chairs were plush and rather fine, reminiscent of a gentleman's club with their dark blue velvets and red velvet cushions. The effect was casually rich, quietly sumptuous. The tiles on the fireplace were Victorian originals and glowed with a rare, dark lustre in the light from the fire.

Of course he could not keep the cat. It was just this one night. The house was not suited to animals, and nor was he. Too much responsibility, too much of a tie. And the mess! Pets were for people who were settled: families and so forth. Despite the house, he did not consider himself settled, even now. Not in that way. Not in the sense of having dependants. So he stayed here, alone, not unhappy, though sometimes longing for large groups of people to descend on him unannounced, so that the house should be full of noise and life. For a day or two.

After a little while he went to bed, shutting the kitten into the kitchen for the night, with a pillowcase stuffed into a cardboard box for a bed. He felt a little pang as he closed the door on that dark fluffy ball of electric life, its flat circular eyes still full of the darkness of birth and danger. He wondered if he should take it up to bed with him. But no, it would soil the bedspread. Besides, he might roll on it in his sleep and crush its matchstick ribs. Reluctantly, he put out the light and went to bed.

He was excited in the morning when he woke. He went quickly down to the kitchen, expectant. When he opened the door he could hear and see nothing at first. Panic! How could such a frail blot of life survive the night all alone! But then he heard a rustling from the corner, and there, in a pile of newspapers, was the kitten, dabbing at some spidery dust clot with its paw. Its eyes were quite mad, and its mouth was half-open, tigerish. He picked it up and gave it another saucer of milk. He glanced round anxiously to see if there were any little stains or pools of urine, but could see nothing. Only the newspapers were a little disarranged – picturesquely so. When he had dressed, he would take it round the houses before work, to find the owners.

He looked at the clock. Ten past eight. Really, there was not enough time, he decided, to take the kitten out before he left for work. No. And he would be disturbing people at their breakfast. Best to leave it till the evening. A little shudder of pleasure went through him then, when he thought of the kitten spending all day in his kitchen and being there when he came home. It was like having a lovely secret. But then he would take it round the houses. He could not possibly keep a cat.

During the day he thought of the kitten often, and the thought warmed him and gave a sprightly zest to his movements. He laughed easily, the pleasure bubbling up with hardly any provocation, and people remarked on it, saying he was looking well. And it was true – he was feeling well, he was looking forward to going home to the kitten. Though God knows what damage it might have wreaked in his kitchen. The creature's energy was out of all proportion to its size.

On his way home he bought some catfood, rather dazzled by the choice in the supermarket. He felt himself for a moment to be part of this new world of cat owners, sharing in their anxieties and affection. But this would be the only tin of catfood he ever bought – a small one, that the kitten would not even finish.

When he got in there was a bit of a mess in the kitchen. It smelled. His kitchen never smelled. And the kitten had walked on the table, and even managed to get up on the worktops – he had been licking the butter! And there was a black hair – a very fine black hair, admittedly – in the sugar bowl.

The man fastidiously tipped the contents of butter dish and sugar bowl into the bin. Now the kitten was not so charming. There followed a great deal of vigorous scrubbing with strong detergent at several pungent stains on the floor and mat. Should he give the kitten more food? That would mean more stains to clean up. The kitten trotted towards him across the kitchen as he bent over his work, its ears and tail alert, its feet prancing as if they danced on tacks. But not so enchanting now – no, not from where the man was standing, a rank smell in his nostrils.

Ten minutes later he was knocking on doors. The kitten clung to his jumper, its eyes wild and desperate-looking. At the first house he went to, nobody was in. At the second and third, he got two women who were kind and polite but knew nothing of the cat. At the fourth he got a miffed young father who told him brusquely that he'd woken the baby. At the fifth house a little girl answered the door and ran off to ask her mummy if they could have the kitten. The mummy said no. At the sixth house was an old man with ancient, heartless eyes. At the seventh was a young executive who already had two cats.

By now it was getting dark and chilly. The kitten was becoming unmanageable, crawling with curious strength from chest to shoulder, to back, to pocket. The man felt the absurdity of his position, but also the friendlessness of the kitten. To be so alone in the world! And so small! And to think it had been stranded in that laurel hedge when he found it . . . and now no-one would take responsibility for it, no-one wanted it. His heart went out to the creature. Already they were connected by their twenty-four hours together. Strange – how quickly attachments formed.

Then he shook himself, mentally. Just a few more houses and the owners would be found. The cat was not his to keep, anyway. Even now some distraught child was probably crying over the lost kitten. He crossed the street and began to work his way down the row of houses.

Twenty minutes later he was back in his own kitchen. The kitten was bleating pitifully, needing food and warmth. The man settled him with a saucer of milk, and another of the new catfood. He made a fresh bed for him in the shoe box. By now it was all quite familiar and cosy. The kitchen looked more lived-in.

When, two days later, a woman came knocking at the door in the evening, and asked if he had found a black kitten of four weeks old, he immediately said no.

After he closed the door he thought – why did I say that? I hadn't made up my mind definitely to keep it. I could go after the woman now, and give the kitten back. But he knew he would not. I have not decided finally, he told himself. And he thought of the mess, and the worry. I can still give him away, or take him to the cat's home, he thought. But this was a mechanical thought, without roots. As soon as he formed it, he realised it was out of the question. Had he chosen to keep the kitten, then?

He went into the kitchen, where he had set up a provisional litter tray near the back door. There was a lid on the butter dish, and a saucer over the sugar bowl. The kitten was swinging from the hem of the tablecloth, a spark of lunatic energy in the otherwise peaceful kitchen. He would have to be taken into consideration now. What a nuisance. But also – what a relief.

CONVALESCENCE

The girl lay on her side, staring at the daffodils. In the red-curtained room, the flowers seemed to be made of stained glass. She stared at them for a long time, blinking slowly, listening to her breathing, peaceful with exhaustion. Life was simplified by illness: the petals of a daffodil became a gift from heaven.

Every so often she moved, shifting the orange glow of her inflamed blood from here to there, taking off the pressure in one place so that it could migrate to somewhere else. She had, for three days and nights, tried every variety of position; she was a choreographer of the sickbed. Flinging her arms above her head sometimes helped, and bending one leg outwards, so that a little coolness could soothe her inner thigh and the undersides of her arms. But nothing lasted. The orange glow returned, this time followed by columns of crawling ants, inching along the pulsating rods of her bones. When she had the strength, she thrashed her head from side to side a few times. There were spots of coolness on the pillow that gave relief that way.

Thoughts of the man came to her as she lay on the bed. She handled the bliss calmly, at this distance. The sharpness had been soothed from her defeat, her humiliation. Now she thought only of those bright, suspended moments when the angel had somehow got inside his breast and was slowly folding and unfolding its furnace-flame wings, like an animal calmly grooming its pelt.

Her mother knocked softly at the bedroom door. Then she appeared, carrying a tray of tea, and set it down by the side of the bed. She was an emissary from the other world, and wore the strange, thoughtless ease of the healthy. How odd, to wear a full set of clothes like that! The girl tried to smile at her mother, and gave up. The tray was another vision, it was radiant with mystery beside her. She let her eyes travel over the china cup and saucer, the silver-grey spoon, the little jug of milk and the great pregnant tea-cosy. It was strange to think of her mother assembling the tray, alone downstairs, in the kitchen that seemed now like an old, loved homeland far away, full of the brightly-lit clutter of objects and radio chatter of normality. How beautiful! And her mother had stood by the kettle, fetching jug and milk and a special cup, and thought about what her daughter would want to drink.The idea moved the girl, to realise this connection between the world of her bedroom, and the world downstairs.

She could not drink the tea, of course. Her mother poured her a cupful, and she could see immediately that it was too strong. Milk would be impossibly rich. She had no desire, no capacity, for food or drink. This must be how Jesus had felt, fasting in the desert for forty days: food had nothing to do with him, the body recoiled from it as from something corrupt.

Her mother subsided, not wishing to tire her with talk. Would she come again? She was going about her own life downstairs, the girl could dimly hear the sounds of doors being opened and shut, of the television starting up, of the lavatory being flushed. Lovely, all of it. Lovely to listen to this life, near to it yet separate.

She had enough energy to be proud of her bed: it was magnificently distraught. It was her creation, her achievement, the unfakeable product of her fever. Her mother had hardly touched it. Sometimes she felt it was like a stage on which she was performing a one-act play. She writhed and tossed and groaned. The stage of suffering, the only place she could be, a pair of watching eyes.

Under her pillow it was still there, the card. She felt for it now, her fingers closing over the vellum and liking its cool smoothness. Would she read it again? Drawing it out, she opened slowly the picture of a single yellow iris, both opulent and chaste. That meant something. It was his way of confessing some tender feeling for her. There inside, his bold, sweeping hand, free of hesitation or remorse. His handwriting had been one of the things she loved; it was something that had travelled with him from the past life she had known nothing about; it was as intimate with him as his fingernails or toes. She traced it with her fingertips, thinking of his hand as he wrote, and the expression on his face, the quiet concentration.

There was a definite fondness in his words. And in the space around the words, as in a silence around speech. The card was the most tender gesture he had offered her. In his leaving, he was full of affection. She could not be bitter and ironical about this: whatever the cause and context, the affection was real. She fed on it like light.

Through the window, snow-glare filled the room with a cold white shock, a pure light like mountain water. The red curtains, half-drawn, filtered and softened it, casting rosy shadows. She lifted her head, and looked out on the up-sloping street, that was carpeted with snow. A blue dazzle glanced off the surface. The birch trees looked patient and resigned, conscripted into the general effect; caterpillars of snow rested along their thin branches. A solitary necklace of footprints strewed the pavement. The houses were capped and dotted and iced and bonneted with blobs of white.

Was it over, then? Ill, she hadn't the energy to mind. But perhaps she did not mind anyway. After the storm, this peacefulness, this return to the basic, spirit-cleansing conflict of cells and microbes, the primitive dramas of the blood. She was still herself, she was returning to herself. The other fever had passed, given way to this, real, bodily fever that would chase it off finally. Her mind, at rest in the moments when clarity descended soft and bright, settled on the memory of his face as it turned to her in some mute confession, his eyes striking softly on her with gentle spears, piercing to the deep dark quick. Over and over she remembered it; and the rest fell away. Of the many truths, she sifted out this one; and those other moments, those other truths, she left to sink away into the yielding earth. The small, radiant tree of his momentary love for her stood proud, would stand always, bearing its single imperishable fruit.

Her mother knew nothing of it, or if she did, said nothing. That was right, too. One must have many worlds, many lives, and not confuse them. There had been her world with him, utterly private and terrifying and marvellous; and there was this, old world, with her mother, to which she was now returned in illness. No need to reconcile them, no need to make them acquainted. But this world was home; the other had been a dream, an exotic escape, a hallucinatory experience, in which everything was intensified, accelerated and dangerous. It was not a place she could inhabit indefinitely. That was why she was relieved and at rest, even though she was wounded. The thing had been done; now it was time for retreat, for the waters to close over once more.

The chill reflections from the street soothed her a little. She watched the slight changes of light on the daffodils. Late snow, in February. And her blood so hot, burning little heaps of coals all over her body. She would not have been surprised to hear that smoke was coming out of her ears. The sheets and blankets were heavy and coarse as hessian, yet she did not want to lie exposed on the bed, either. So she lay half-covered with a tangle of cotton and wool, pushing it away, then dragging it over her legs once more, turning onto her stomach and thrusting her arms under the pillows, then curling into a sea-horse on her side, attempting sleep which came only lightly and fitfully, a gauzy curtain which still let in the wind.

WONDERS OF NATURE

It was one of the first real spring days. The breeze was stiff but there was a mildness in the air, and the fields and hedgerows shone yellow and green. A new freshness sprang from everything, an energy of young life. There were sudden rashes of daffodils by the roadside, and little starry celandines everywhere. The young couple, driving out of the city for a proper Sunday jaunt, were delighted with it all. 'Look!' the woman kept saying, 'look!' – and she would point to a crop of wild irises, or a horse starting madly and playfully in a field. It was a perfect day for a walk.

She was a nature poet. Not that she had deliberately set out to write nature poetry; but now, after two collections in which birds, flowers, trees, and the exquisite changes of light on distant hills figured so largely, it was plain that this was what she was, and more than one reviewer had dubbed her 'Wordsworthian'. For those who liked her poetry, she was a great relief after the obscure and tortuous morbidities of the contemporary scene – all those poets obsessed with ugliness and violence. No, after them, she was refreshing as a bunch of just-picked wildflowers. A child-like wonder ran through her work; a simple delight in the manifold beauties of nature. And after all, her admirers would say a little defensively, what was wrong with that?

Her husband parked the car in a lay-by right in the heart of the countryside. They liked to get as far away as possible from the big roads. And fifty yards back they had seen a crooked sign marked 'walkers' path', pointing across the fields. Now they found it again – though there was no discernible path, in fact; just a knobbly, sheep-cropped field, a line of old oaks and a small, half-hidden stream. Charming, though – just what they wanted, really. The smell of the grass in their nostrils, the spring of the turf under their feet. And the air full of birdsong, like a delicate rushwork of tiny threads.

'Look!' said the poet, before they had got very far. She was pointing to something invisible near her feet.

'What have you found?' said her husband, who knew her talent for finding unusual flowers, and liked to share her enthusiasms.

'It's germander speedwell,' she told him, stooping to the grass and turning up the tiny face of the flower with one delicate fingertip. They gazed at it together. 'So pretty!'

'Tiny!' They didn't pick it, of course.

'God, it's good to get away – properly away,' said the husband, beginning to breathe deeply at last, with the steepening field and the uneven ground. The air was like a fresh mountain stream after the foul, polluted city streets. He worked in an office all week, on the council. He shared his wife's love of nature, though realised he was not as quiveringly sensitive as she.

'Look!' She had seen something else. There was always so much to notice with her. It was like going out with a young child who had never seen real sheep and cows. She was pointing to a nondescript clump of brambles.

'A pheasant – behind there!' They crept up to the brambles and peeped behind. Nothing. Then a muffled scurry. 'Can you see him?' she whispered. Her eyes were bright as a startled deer. But the bird was infuriatingly shy and reluctant to be admired. They left him, rather dolefully.

'How far shall we go?' said the husband.

'Oh, I think at least to the end of the next field, don't you?'

It really was a glorious day. Wordsworth would have felt his soul expanding. 'Isn't it marvellous?' burst out the husband suddenly, flinging his arms wide as if to take in the great vastness of the sky and fields and distant hills. His wife, privately, was rather embarrassed by these displays of exuberance: there was something just a little forced, she felt. But she stood, smiling patiently, looking appreciative, until he had drunk his fill of the general glory, and was ready to stride on.

They came to the next field. Here there were many sheep, with their new lambs. Oh, how small they were, and full of life! Their little woolly limbs, so rounded and eager, were like the drawings on a nursery wall. 'Oh, look!' cried the poet, as she took in this new joy.

'Aren't they darlings?' said the husband.

A breeze caught his hat then, and bowled it off across the field towards a ragged line of wire fencing, where it stuck by a little thorn tree. He lumbered after it, and she followed. Then, as he was bending to retrieve it, 'Oh, look!' she said. And there was a little lamb, standing alone by the thorn, looking as if it was stuck between the tree and the fence. Except it was not trying to escape; it just stood there, rather dazed and lost, its umbilical cord still hanging like a thread of crimson cotton from its belly.

'Oh you poor thing! Are you lost then?' The poet's tenderness intensified to unbearable poignancy; all her maternal protectiveness flowed forth. As she looked closer, she saw there was something not quite right about the lamb. It had a shaved, half-finished look, as if its coat was not properly grown in places, and the pink, vulnerable skin showed through. And its face was more than usually nubby, its eyes rather listless and red-rimmed. 'Oh you poor thing! You've lost your mum!'

'He's new-born,' said the husband, and there was a shadow in his voice.

'Here, hold this,' said his wife, handing him her knapsack, and going round the fence to where the lamb was stalled. She began to usher the little creature back into the field. But he staggered slowly and uncertainly.

She had to pick him up and carry him the last yards. 'Oh darling, are you sure you can manage?' The husband had a slightly suffering look on his face. He watched as his wife trotted a little way towards a group of sheep and lambs, hunched over her rather heavy foundling.

But the other sheep just stood four-square and stared blankly, or sloped off, showing no interest.

'There we are! There we are!' The woman was putting down the lamb now, delivering it back to its family, as she thought. But none of the sheep seemed to want it. The husband winced; it really was a pathetic sight.

When his wife turned to him, there were the beginnings of tears in her eyes. She looked rather desperate.

'Oh dear, oh dear!'

The lamb looked even more lost now than before, in the middle of the wide-open field, so nakedly and cruelly alone. He shivered a little, and simply stood, quite still, unable to help himself. There was something stupid and half-formed in his long, bony legs, that seemed not to know what to do. The other sheep went back to their cropping and took no notice of him.

'I'm afraid it sometimes happens,' said the husband, coming up close to his grieving wife. 'Mothers abandon their lambs, and the farmers have to adopt them, or make another ewe take them.'

It was too awful. How could they walk away? Surely

the right mother would appear at any moment, and the lamb would leap joyfully towards her, bleating. But the creature stood there, still and silent, sunk in some darkness of inertia. It was as if he had not properly woken up.

'We can't leave him,' said the poet.

'We could try finding the farmer,' said the husband, distressed by his wife's grief. Her eyes were wet with tears of pity and frustration.

'I suppose so. Oh, the poor thing! What will happen to him?'

A pair of magpies broke heavily from a tree overhead. Their wings were huge and brilliant, their beaks like picks.

'I'm sure the farmer will find him,' said the husband. 'It's very common.' But he was not convinced. They would go to the nearby houses and tell someone about the lamb. Yes, that was the answer.

But they could not find the farm. After crawling in the car along the lanes for half a mile, he turned to her and said, 'We could go back, and look in the other direction – if you'd like?'

But they both knew they wouldn't. She stared out of the window at the rolling fields. There was something her spirit could not digest, an alien object. Only time and distance would help.

That night her husband said, 'Will you write a poem about it?' He imagined she would write something, not quite in her usual style – more harsh, more naked and disturbing.

But she answered quickly, 'Oh no! I couldn't write a poem about that.'

It was true. And for weeks she wrote nothing, not a line.

BURIED TREASURE

Hillcrest Gardens was secreted from the street by a narrow entrance, so that a casual glance would tell you nothing was there except another grand old house, hidden by the usual bulwark of conifers. You really had to be looking for it if you wanted to find it – and even then you might easily walk past because you'd missed the little curved pieces of doll-sized railing painted dark green; or because you thought once again, no! it's not that turning! I always make the mistake of thinking it is! And strolling on.

Bethan Thomas actually thought the park had been removed when she returned after twenty-five years to see her old playground again. Her idea now, in her thirty-fourth year, was to revisit all the places of her childhood, and perhaps to paint them, for she was a modestly successful artist. Already she had retraced her daily journey to junior school, from the first house where she had lived, down the old streets and gulleys where she had skated on the icy paving stones on winter mornings, and swung like a monkey from the safety bars placed at the exits from the gulleys. The visit had filled her with strange feelings – not quite those she had expected. For everything had altered from her memory of it; and this interfered with her pleasure in recalling her childhood, for after that she had the sense that she might be making a lot of it up.

But Hillcrest Gardens would not have changed. Even as an eight-year-old Bethan had foreseen her own nostalgia for this little park that seemed, even then, to be known by hardly anyone. Her mother had taken her there – it was too far for her to visit alone – and it had always been empty, except for the occasional dog walker, and once, in July, a group of white-trousered old men playing bowls.

Yes, her intuition had been right. This was the entrance, by the white wall and the camellia hedge, which was in full blossom and shedding great splashes of dark pink petals on the pavement. Bethan followed the upward-sloping, anonymous path, half expecting to find herself in someone's front yard. Then, as she crested the slope, the path opened out and there before her were the old gates, just as she remembered them, wrought iron in two kissing scrolls, with the name of the park traced across the curling top.

Sure enough, there was nobody here. A whiff of hot blossom drifted from the gardens. Tarmac under her feet glittered and softened in the sun. Ahead she could see a high tunnel of yew and cypress hedges – another secretive entrance. Bethan felt her heart lift. It was almost too much to hope for, that nothing had changed.

As she came into the garden proper, she began to

recall more and more. This was where she had roller-skated with her mother, following the curve of the path round to the right; and that was where they had fallen on the grass more than once. There were the bowling greens, of course, spartan and untouchable, closed off from the public; oh, and the summer house! How could she have forgotten that! It had a little water spout inside, that you could drink from on hot days.

But something was missing. Although the park enchanted her with its ghosts and memories – subtly altered from her recollections, but that was part of the charm – she knew that she had not got to the heart of the mystery. Any minute now she would come upon it, she knew. It was that one special place, the one that held the key to her childhood experience of this park as magical, shining with the essence of indefinable promise and joy.

She walked on, past the grove of birches, over the tiny footbridge that now seemed twee rather than quaint, and up the brick path to the bird house, where three lilac-winged budgerigars perched and squawked in Stygian gloom. She hurried away from them.

Looking out across the back of the park, where a bank of grass sloped down to a line of sycamores, beyond which was the sun-hazed horizon of the suburbs, Bethan wondered if she would bring her paints and brushes here and do a series of miniatures – all the mysterious secret little turnings and twists of the park. This was what she had envisaged before she came. Illustrations for a book of poems, perhaps – sonnets by Rilke, for instance.

But something was missing. It was as if she walked through a set of beautiful rooms in which the lights had not been switched on. She was expecting the blaze. She knew it was waiting for her – possibly just round the next corner – because she remembered it from twenty-five years before. She would not have returned otherwise.

She passed a woman with a corgi on a long lead. The dog stopped to sniff Bethan's leg. The woman jerked the dog away, unsmiling. Bethan's placatory smile was left to dissolve unseen on the warm, thin summer air. A family of sparrows cheeped noisily from a nearby bush. Bethan strayed towards them, thinking, yes! I remember that bush! If I just turn that corner I will find it! And she almost crept up on the bush, as if to take by surprise whatever it concealed, before it bolted.

But the bush concealed nothing. To her dismay Bethan realised the path now rejoined the place where she had come into the park – there was no more to see. That was it. But I know there is more, she thought, feeling intensely frustrated. It all looked so much smaller than she remembered it, and so much more manicured. And – she hated to admit it – but the park was rather dull. You could do the circuit in ten minutes, really. And there was far too much tarmac. No wonder hardly anyone ever walked here.

As she left, she even wondered if she had got the right park. Could she have made a mistake? For this was certainly not the same place she had known when she was eight. They must have changed it. Yes, that was it.

THE LAST LETTER

Oh, the rain in the streets that night! And where, where was she going? Out of the house, out, anywhere, away from the letter, the burning, molten letter with its exit marks still smoking in the pit of her stomach. She must run from it, run from those words, their annihilating clarity. Out into the streets where the rain was sweeping in grey, receding veils, ceaselessly, tirelessly, splashing onto the black pavements and twining bright, fast threads in the gutters. She banged the door behind her and she ran, ran like she had a train to catch, out into the darkness where the night and the rain knew nothing of the letter – where the words could not follow her.

When she thought of the contrast: how each of his other letters had set her dreaming for days; had given her imagination banquets to feed on, as she lovingly turned over each phrase a dozen times, letting it explode again on her consciousness like a beautiful firework, spreading warm sparks through her veins. His letters. Even the weather had known of them. The birds, the trees, the air itself sang with approval, echoing her secret joy. She told no-one. She showed no-one. But the letters opened and re-opened inside her, twenty times a day, and each morning when she woke she knew there was some great surprise waiting for her – yes! It was the thought of his last letter, that she had not reread in memory since the night before.

But now, the rain came down harder, so hard she thought it must be near to spending itself completely, and would soon stop. But it did not stop. For which she was grateful, because the sound satisfied something in her. And she was drenched, extravagantly wet, with even her underwear, she felt, cold and clinging to her wet body. There was no sense in trying to stay dry, no use for an umbrella or hat. She strode on through the black, shiny, yellow-beaconed streets, not knowing where she was going, but certain that she could not return to the house yet.

She had left the letter in her room. She had scrunched it up into a ball in a fury of misery and humiliation, and thrown it in the bin. The words had been bladed, like long flashing swords. When she opened the letter – so innocent-looking! as if it were not a magic box of knives – she had clutched the page stiffly, and read with tense, staring eyes, hardly able to look at the page. She read very quickly, knowing beforehand what it would say, and just needing to be sure. Yes, she was sure. Her eyes winced rapidly down the page, retrieving a word here, a phrase there, a 'sorry', a 'mistake', a 'friendship'. Her breath was coming hard now. The letter was a falsehood, an impertinence. She would not subject herself to it. Shaking, she glanced quickly at the signature – 'Yours sincerely, Francis' – and crushed the paper in her hand, flinging it from her. Alien tissue. Inadmissible. The iron brand going in deep, instantaneous, searing her brain. She must get out.

The rain helped her. She began to moan, and the sound of the rain absorbed it. When the wind whipped up she even wailed, a little gasp of a wail at first, slightly self-conscious, then a louder cry, from the pit of her stomach. The rain snatched it up and dashed it on the ground. She hunched and dragged on, past the dark, oblivious houses, past the dripping trees and the streaming gutters, the wet brick walls and the cars sending up fans of spray.

Now she wanted to get as wet as possible. Her hot cheeks and salty eyes, disguised by darkness and the weather, she did not try to hide. Besides, there was no-one in the streets. And the night was moonless, more black than she had ever known it. How far had she come? Not far enough. Behind her, in the basket, the letter smouldered, its branding-irons still hot and smoking.

'A misunderstanding!' The worst word of all! She crumpled again, winded, as she recalled it now. For a moment she stopped, panting, by a wall, and put a hand out to lean on. Oh, the shame, the ineradicable torment of knowing his boredom and displeasure. Not just guessing it, nor suspecting it, but knowing it. The awkwardness she had caused him – the irritation! And his letters? His kisses? She could not fathom it – would not. All was cancelled, all annulled. And now must be sunk fast in a deep pit, quick, before its shape and colour and the texture of its skin became something she took in forever, and could not dismiss from memory.

The rain beat down, not letting up. She grew cold; her shoulders felt as if a cold wind blew on them. She was aware of a squelching in her shoes. The street lights snaked ahead, curving over the brow of the hill. She lifted her head and saw how far they stretched. She limped on for some yards, then paused, and shuddered. She looked back. The rain was sweeping in ghostly scarves across the dark, submissive privet hedges and gardens. She looked again in the other direction. She had come as far as she wanted to. But she could not go back yet; not yet.

A WALK IN GLADSTONE GARDENS

The ladies of Coed Mor were a sturdy and spirited lot. They were women who had outlived their husbands or never had one; women freed in the last portion of their lives to return to a version of girlhood, when company was the company of friends and laughter was the currency of that friendship.

For it was remarkable how much these women laughed. Young lovers, passing a small cluster of them on the esplanade or pier, would be taken aback at the hoots and cackles, great gusts of merriment quivering the genteel air of the seaside town. The women looked like their nans looked; they had white, gold, or pale blue perms, wore glasses, and were dressed in outfits from British Home Stores: floral print dresses, lacy cardigans and wide-fitting shoes. Their faces were rosy and weather-toughened or small and sharp; their figures likewise too fat or too thin. They had, in short, put on the uniform of the old; not, though, in a slavish conformity, but because they came of a class and generation that saw no reason to question tradition, no shame in looking alike, and who therefore dressed and wore their hair now as their mothers and aunts had done before them.

They had their chosen territory within the town. It consisted of the area around the Carnegie library, the grocery shops behind the high street, and on Sundays in particular, the seafront with its Edwardian esplanade and robustly decorated pier. In these places they congregated, when they were not paying each other home visits or passing each other at the hairdresser's. Certain teashops were favoured – The Happy Hearth was old-fashioned and unpretentious, sold good strong tea and decent macaroons; Luigi's on the seafront was where they sometimes took refuge on Sundays when it rained. Sundays were for ice-creams, though: vanilla cornets from a stall on the pier, a rather shocking price, but it was proper dense yellow ice-cream in a crisp sugar cone.

The places they did not frequent were the parks. This was not just because both the parks were situated picturesquely on steep inclines, hard on their muscles and bones, but because they were unsafe. One might find oneself alone in a park, out of earshot of help, and with no door to bolt against intruders. Chestnut trees and rosebeds were no use in a crisis; a view of the sea would offer no stay of execution. Comfort, if not safety, lay in numbers for the ladies. The stories they had heard would not bear repeating. But they would not be paddocked in their own small quarters by fear; and so they went around together, if not by deliberate design then by unspoken agreement that this, after all, was what women their age must do.

This avoidance of the parks was a pity, because Gladstone Gardens in particular was a magical place, structured on several tiers linked by a series of long sloping paths and small flights of stone steps that gave the stroller a delightful sense of participating in a secret game. The invisible presence of those who had conceived and built the looping walkways and high grass banks, the grove of lilac trees and the miniature bridge leading to the fountain; the arborealist who had known where the perfect place was to plant the pine trees to frame the view of the sea from the top of the park; the gardener who had placed coral-coloured camellia bushes in a rarely-visited recess, so that whoever stumbled on them felt it was a private discovery; these things combined to make Gladstone Gardens unique not just in the town, but in the city to which it was attached. Not that it was a famous park in the Kew Gardens style. There was nothing ostentatious or eccentric about it; nor would you find any rare exotic flora there (though there was a rather lovely Judas tree that in May and June sprouted hot pink blossoms from its trunk). Rather, it was one of those local treasures, loved alike by residents who passed through it on their way to and from work every day, and by weekend walkers, solitaries and lovers, friends and young families who came to drink at its cup for an hour, to be renewed by its green seclusion and quiet delights.

It was a fine day in September when Ivy Bevan, one of the ladies of Coed Mor, decided to hell with it, she was going to walk through the park on her own. Over the years she had got into the habit, instinctively, of avoiding it, as had her friends. Today however there was no-one to accompany Ivy – both Margaret and Eileen were being taken out by relatives, and Nora was laid up with a touch of bronchitis – and she was damned if she was going to miss the best of the day. Having a special fondness for trees, she liked to follow their cycle of flowering and decay from April to October; and Gladstone Gardens held some very fine maples that, in the autumn months, turned a rich ruddy gold and shed great sharp stars of colour on the grass. This display lasted for only a couple of weeks, however. So Ivy set out, carrying her purse and keys strapped to her waist under her cardigan, as she had been advised to do on such occasions, and wearing her woollen winter coat since there was now a nip in the air. At first, all went well. She passed a couple with a dog coming out of Gladstone Gardens as she was going in, and further on, a father with two small girls. These signs of ordinariness reassured her. She walked slowly along the park's main avenue that was lined with bright coppery chestnut trees, past the bandstand, down the steps to the slightly dingy aviary, then towards the lower slopes where the maples were. The sky was a brilliant blue, the colour of a Chinese vase; but there was a stiff breeze, and tufts of low cloud bowled along rapidly overhead.

It was as she was emerging from the shelter of the aviary that she saw them: three boys, wearing back-to-front baseball caps and crouching over something on the ground under a sycamore tree. Immediately Ivy began to turn in the other direction, feeling her blood cool. She did not know what the boys were doing and she did not wish to know. It might be a bird; it might be drugs. Her strongest instinct, like that of a hedgehog interrupted in its saucer of milk, was to bolt. Except that, being eighty-two, the best she could manage was a purposeful totter.

It was too late, however. The boys had seen her, and they smelt a quarry.

There was no shouting. No cat-calling or baiting. Instead, an ominous silence, then a murmuring, and another pause during which Ivy heard only the shuffle of her own progress, and felt eyes boring into her back.

It was all over in less than thirty seconds. At the end of it Ivy was left buckled up in a laurel bush – she remembered afterwards the sharp scent – looking up at the China blue sky.

'Don't struggle, they might get violent,' she had been told; and amazingly, she had remembered the advice and gone limp as a sleeping cat while the boys frisked her and removed her purse – with all of £7.50 in it. She had shut her eyes so as not to see their faces.

Now she was alone again. She began to extricate herself from the bush and check herself for bruises and strains. She cautiously flexed her fingers, probed her waist where the boys had ripped off the purse, tested the strength of her legs. Her legs were in fact watery, but that was only natural and would correct itself in a minute. Ivy adjusted her hat, her clothes, rebuttoned her coat, picked up her brolly where it had got dropped during the fracas, and after a few minutes' rest, began to walk on again towards the maple trees.

She was shaken all right. But the worst had come, and she had survived it; and therefore some exhilaration also attended her on the rest of her walk through the park. Even when she passed a young family who seemed the very essence of safety and decency, she made no appeal to them, did not collapse on them and tell her tale. There was a split second, it is true, when she thought she might – just as the woman was passing with her little girl, and gave Ivy a friendly smile – but Ivy simply straightened her back, gave a polite nod, and walked on.

The maples were splendid. Never had she seen them so majestic and glossily abundant. A dark fiery lustre glowed from the deep layers of leaves, and the grass below was thickly strewn with huge splashes of leathery maroon and tawny yellow. One leaf that she stooped to pick up was a whole rainbow of reds, golds and greens, and this one she pocketed, even though she knew it would be curled and dry before nightfall.

Ivy stood under the maples. The trees fluttered above her softly like draped awning. She stood there for a long time. She was thinking of how she would tell

Eileen about the trees tomorrow at the hairdresser's, and Eileen would say, 'You never went to the park alone!' And Ivy would say she did, and what's more, no harm came to her, and she would go again. And then they would change the subject, and there would be laughter – great gusts of it – as they shared their gossip, and talked about the old days, and remembered how strict their mothers had been with them when they were girls, giving them hell if they came in late on a Saturday night, because everyone knew what *that* meant.

THEY ALSO SERVE

The young man dined alone that night in the hotel restaurant. It was a cavernous basement room without windows, decked out fussily with ruched floral curtains and miniature brass lamps. The hotel staff – youngsters with gawky limbs protruding from cheap uniforms, barracked there for the summer – steered him to a table so devoid of charm and comfort he thought for a moment of objecting. That morning at breakfast he had innocently sat at a table reserved for another couple and been gracelessly moved on. It was not the first time since he had arrived that he had shown his ignorance of the rules and been stared at by more seasoned guests. He felt like the new boy at school, where only after many years would he be accepted and absorbed.

He was not in fact young. A month before, he had passed his thirty-ninth birthday. His face had altered in the last few years from its usual softness and high colour to a slightly strained and faded nubbiness. His skull was now visible under the skin, and his eyes seemed lost and taken aback. But he had never stopped thinking of himself as young, and nor had others. His temperament and demeanour, his mild and unassuming innocence, ensured that. He would be a boyish old man, too, sprightly and harmless, performing wholesome and quiet duties.

The waitress wrote down his order. He took in, briefly, the radiance of her young face, her slim brown hands. She was plainly bored, and recited the choice of starters with indecent haste. Unable to bring himself to ask her to repeat it, he chose the last thing she mentioned. There was a small tattoo of a bluebird on her right wrist, and he kept his eyes on this while she took the rest of his order. When she left she gave him a strange look and blushed.

He told himself that he had been right to come on holiday alone. It was not the first time, anyway. And it did not have to become a habit. But for many years now he had lived alone, and grown little by little into the routines of a solitary life. In his home town he could be seen on Sundays doing the coastal walk, his small neat rucksack strapped to his back, his cheeks fresh in the wind. In another age he would have been a country parson.

He got out his book. It was a novel by Herman Hesse. He read one paragraph – about a boy sitting an algebra exam in intense summer heat – then put it aside. He had never mastered the art of reading in public, and always felt like an actor on a stage, fooling no-one. He ventured a look at the other diners. There was nobody immediately next to him – the waiter had put him, humiliatingly, on a little island at the far end of the room – but two tables away a silent and lugubrious family of four were industriously working their way through large platefuls of chicken and chips. It was remarkable how little they said to each other. The mother put down her knife and fork now and then and looked at her son, and made some gentle enquiry of him – he ignored her – but the others seemed bound in a compact of companiable silence, as if talking were a practice they had long ago abandoned and decided never to revive.

This exposure of private family habits was of great interest to the man who sat alone. It cheered him that the family ate in silence, though he was not sure why. He watched as the father asked barely audibly for the salt, and the daughter passed it, graciously but mechanically. They functioned as a unit, the four of them, almost by telepathic signals. The meal was a task, jointly shouldered. The food was familiar food, reliable. They ate here every night.

The family did not look at the young man. They were not curious in that way. But he became conscious of some attention from a young couple seated on his other side, whose snatched glances and huddled, hushed exchanges made him shrink a little. They were giggling. The boy had his hand on the girls's knee under the table and was staring boldly into her face, murmuring something that made her cheeks flame and her eyes shine. She protested, and glanced quickly at the solitary young man, then exploded with half-stifled laughter. He looked away.

His first course came, and he ate it neatly and quickly. He was hungry after his day's walking. Driven from his room early by the hot sun, he had wandered the town from top to bottom, idling in cool bookshops and visiting the church that had a fine Tudor ceiling studded with heraldic symbols. There was a time when such things would not have interested him, but now he sought out old things and took pleasure in running his hands over ancient stone fonts, and puzzling at fragments of medieval crosses and the inscriptions on Jacobean gravestones. The reconciliation of past and present in these churches soothed him. The smell of beeswax polish on the pews, the lilies and chrysanthemums in tall vases on the window ledges, and the gentle clatter of activity from the vestry, where elderly ladies served cheap and delicious tea and cakes – these things sat well with the cold smell of centuries-old stone, and the dusty brilliance of the crowded little stained-glass windows. It soothed him, and he found himself seeking out the oldest church in every new village he visited now, always hopeful of this combination of domesticity and mystery.

When his fish pie arrived, he saw at once it was made with instant mash and the cheapest woolly-blanket coley, and dispatched it without ceremony. There was a bone, which he placed tidily on the rim of his plate. The family of four were leaving, pushing back their chairs in unison and gathering up cardigans and keys, having demolished vast quantities of food. The father had great hairy bare legs like tree trunks, and rather finely-shaped sun-browned feet in open sandals. The young man had changed out of his own shorts for dinner; the nudity of strangers – even the bare legs – was something he had never quite stopped being shocked by.

The family had a busy and disciplined air, as if they were on a well-planned mission with no room for spontaneous digressions. By comparison, the young man felt wispy and unfocused. He had no plans on this holiday, he had decided to go where the mood took him, and be open to surprises. But now he was wondering whether it wouldn't be better if he had an aim, an objective; an air of purpose would at least shield him from the attention of oddballs.

He would make a systematic tour of the coast, he decided. Yes, that was it. Not the usual tourist spots; not the boat ride to the wildlife reserve or the visit to the ruined abbey; but his own itinerary, eccentric and adventurous. He would take the low roads, the side tracks, the secret deserted alleyways where nobody walked because they led from nowhere to nowhere. He would get out his Ordnance Survey map and investigate barrows and burial mounds, Norman churches and quiet pubs where the cool gloom would enfold him after the burning sunshine. There would be streams where the cow parsley and angelica had grown so high on the banks that he would wade through them shoulder-high. He would see unusual birds – a kingfisher, perhaps, or a kestrel. Then he would come across a stretch of thistled field next to a wood, a place where he could lie down in the grass and drink tea from a thermos, read his book and feel the sun on his neck as he listened to the buzzing of insects in the holy quiet. On the way back he would notice a rusted tangle of old farm machinery, sitting majestically in the long grass, next to an empty, rotting shed. All these things he would store and remember; this would be his holiday.

The bored waitress with the beautiful hands brought him his dessert. She served him quickly and unceremoniously, and he reddened when he remembered her blush. The dessert was three kinds of ice-cream, golfball-sized scoops heaped in a glass dish, with some pallid chunks of tinned fruit salad strewn round the edges. He ate with quiet intentness, shaving off melting strips of the ice-cream and spooning them deftly, almost rhythmically, into his mouth. He didn't look up until he had finished and lain his empty dish aside. Then he rose, decisively, and left the restaurant.

The night was balmy indigo. Scents of rose and buddleia came up fom the gardens, mingling with the salt breeze from the sea. He walked to the end of the esplanade, then down the wooden ramp to the beach, where a little light from the street above lit his way along the shoreline. The tide was high and still coming in fast; he was alone on the beach, everyone else was in the bars and nightclubs of the town, or just sitting down to late meals. On one side he could hear the indistinct hubbub of voices and music, the pulse of the disco; on the other the swish and drag of the ocean waves, so wild and yet so close.

In the darkness, his aloneness no longer worried him. The sea made no judgement on it, the cliffs were indifferent, absorbed in their own mass and height. For a while he became unconscious of himself, aware only of the sound his shoes made on the soft grains, and the coolness of his cheek where the sea air played on it. He was no longer young. He would not marry now, and this was the first of many holidays he would spend on his own. He knew this, not in his conscious thoughts, but in his bones. Somehow he had grown into the pattern of himself – habits and forms of life that were as unchosen and unalterable as his thumbprint.

A friend had tried to change him once. She had invited him to socials and dinner parties where he might meet women; had urged him to join the Ramblers and an evening class in conversational French. She had even come shopping with him for clothes that were brighter and snappier than the things he usually wore. He had played along with her, to please her. But at the end of every social evening, at the close of each class, his old solitude waited for him like a much-worn comfortable coat moulded to the shape of his shoulders.

He stooped to pick up something from the sand. It was a child's toy, a small plastic doll wearing a bathing suit. He took it to the edge of the wooden ramp at the top of the beach and propped it up in the greenery on the hedged wall that skirted the ramp, where the owner might see it tomorrow. Then he toiled back up towards the lamplit street, turning up his collar against the stiffening breeze. A straggle of noisy youths turned from the street down to the beach then, and he walked towards them, not slackening his step or making way for them, but keeping to his middle path steadily, so that when they drew level they parted for him like water, and passed on.

SUMMER INTERLUDE

It was one of those summer mornings that come as an unexpected portent of autumn: after weeks of sun, it had now rained in the night, and the household woke to a glimmering grey light and the sad feeling that an end had been declared to their holiday. Mrs Cranham, splashing her face with water in the bathroom, looked out on the long field of the garden and saw her husband's spade, still stuck in the earth after his digging yesterday, now jewelled with raindrops. Her daughter Felicity, fifteen, lay in bed a little longer, and longed for the days as a child when her father had carried a first cup of tea up to her room in the mornings. She wished to wake slowly, not stirring yet from the hive of warm blankets, and to contemplate the changes of light and temperature, looking from her window, propped up against her pillows and silently sipping hot tea. She decided to dash down and make herself a cup, then bring it back up. No tennis today, by the look of it. But Robbie was coming home from his European trip. It was fitting that the weather should be so British.

Mr Cranham emerged from his bedroom in the dark red Shetland-wool dressing gown with satin cord trim on the cuffs, tassels on the belt. His slippers were Italian leather. The rest of him was by now rather shakily put together, so it was all the more important to have decent gear. He descended the stairs with his usual panting breath, disguising it and cheering himself by half whistling, as if he were going about some carpentry or mending work. He made his tea very deliberately, though his hands were not entirely steady, and looked out sharply into the garden with an air of assessment, as if he were still in army uniform and calculating the chances of crossing a crucial piece of terrain. What he saw was next door's cat dancing lightly across the lawn, picking up her feet to keep them dry. And further down, a robin perched on the handle of his spade. His son Robbie was due home today.

His wife shuffled languidly into the kitchen, a bundle of crumpled elegance in her Chinese-silk peignoir, beaded slippers and faded gold hair slipping like an undercooked meringue from the loose coils on her head. She had a slovenly beauty, and like her husband smoked a cigarette with the morning tea, her long sensitive fingers draped over painted porcelain and dusky tangerine silk. Her face, still puzzled by sleep, had a faint pink flush at this hour and the skin was soft. Her lazy eyes, the colour of dark chocolate, were at their most beautiful, having no designs on anybody and still half scarfed in night.

The kitchen was filled with the melancholy glints of an overcast summer morning, and the sighs and murmurs of bodies not yet risen from the infantilising cocoon of oblivion. A spoon stirring tea, knocked against the side of a cup, gently replaced in a saucer; the rasp of a match taking light; the first long exhalation of smoke, and fingers of blue cloud dreaming upwards from the lit cigarette; these were what Felicity met with as she crossed the kitchen without ceremony, a creature with dazzled eyes and the softest of narrow white feet wincing from the tiled floor. Tea in the pot? Yes, and hot water in the kettle: her father's thoroughness in small matters. She passed by the familiar silent colloquy of the kitchen table, where her parents nursed their separate bruised awakenings, and a small halo of smoke settled above their heads like the last fumes of sleep. Then it was up, up the stairs, quickly, before the bed cooled, and back into the oven of the sheets, to lie propped against pillows and consider the darkness of the cypresses outside her window, and the snakes of rain strewn brightly on the little flat roof.

Mrs Cranham switched on the lights in the house that morning, and it was like getting up early in winter while it was still dark. Some washing left out on the line the night before was now hanging disconsolate and heavy, wet through. She brought it in before she went up to her bath. She would take her time bathing today – consolation for the dark weather – and take her time dressing, too. Alright if I use the bathroom first? This to Mr Cranham, ensconced like a Victorian patriarch at the table, surrounded by the accoutrements of a civilised breakfast: large unwieldy newspaper, willow-pattern breakfast cup full of steaming oxblood tea; ashtray, matches and untipped Players Navy Cut. The post? Ah yes – a letter from Violet, in spidery copperplate, on pale blue Basildon Bond. No news, because there never was any; but the usual enquiries and the usual complaints about her hip and knee. Oh, and an unopened letter for Felicity, in an unfamiliar hand, tiny, as if done by an ant dipped in black ink. What time was Robbie due? Plenty of time yet. He belonged to the far continent of the afternoon.

And now Mrs Cranham is running her bath and yes – humming as she does so, because when else can you hum if not when waiting for the bath to fill? – and she stoops to hold a long hand under the hot tap, checking the temperature, and is pleased as always by the lucent swell of greenish water deepening under the head of oily foam. The silent pleasures of purification! Off slides the Chinese-silk peignoir, off she kicks the beaded slippers; above the steaming bath of water she hovers, enjoying the naked dryness of her skin, the heavy breasts and smooth, pale loins. Then into the water, first one foot then the other, and the glove of warmth sheathes her to the neck. Her nipples break the surface of the water like small volcanic islands, her toes, already pink, flex and rub at the deliciously cold brass taps. Here she lets herself float, half buoyed, while the perfumed water evaporates like the freakish lakes of Iceland, and the window quickly clouds its eye with steam. For minutes there are no sounds but the secret, intimate drippings and swirlings of water, the lazy stirrings of the hot green lake.

Now Felicity stirs also from her nest of early morning reflections and feels the chilly clasp and command of the hardening day. Up! Up and about! Dispel this gloomy enchantment and break open the morning, tear off the creeping cobwebs of dusky summer rainclouds. The nipping air helps, and the new cool clarity of the washed atmosphere. Into sandals and linen trousers, into a thin sweater. Cool silk of hair brushed quickly with fierce strokes – there, done. Face slapped with cold water, cheeks fresh and pink. Teeth brushed, quick, gobbet of minty foam swilled down little bedroom sink. Mouth fresh, tingling. Hands washed, soft, pink and cool. Ready now, ready for whatever waits. What? What is to be done with the sombre, recalcitrant morning? Her father still smokes and sips his tea below, crackling the great thin wings of the paper, turning the pages like maps of the world. The clock in the hall ticks, solidly, seems almost to stop between ticks: surely that is longer than a second? The relentless, comforting, indifferent passing of time. Steady, unstoppable. It clothes the dark, dignified silence of the hall, where no sun has come today, and will not come now.

But Robbie will come. Galloping and howling, like a dog at the gate. Robbie will arrive out of the silent, overcast sky, in the dead hour of the July afternoon when the trees are all gone to sleep, and there is the somnolent lull before the stirring towards evening. Robbie with his bright hair and ragged clothes hanging negligently from bronzed skin and long limbs, like a medieval minstrel, ready to snatch up a piccolo or a fiddle and fill the air with coloured music . . . Robbie will be home. And he will play a game of tennis with Felicity on the back lawn, though there is no net. And he will embrace his mother with gusto and remark that she looks tired but beautiful . . . and Mr Cranham will clasp his shoulder and utter some awkward, well-considered words. Then Robbie will scoop up the passing cat, their latest, called Butler after Rhett Butler in *Gone with the Wind* because he is dashing and doesn't give a damn, and make him walk across the back of his shoulders and feel his claws in his scalp, so delicious and tantalising. Then there will be a pause, an hour or two when the pulse of the day slows again, and shadows begin to gather in the garden under the louring cypresses, and Mrs Cranham commandeers the kitchen, listening to the radio while she chops and slices and boils and bastes. And presently, as Felicity and Robbie lie splayed in the living room, admiring their browned limbs or leaping up for a sudden duet on the piano, the aromas of roast lamb and rosemary, of hot crisping potatoes and blueberry tart, will circle them in the room, and they will exchange a look that says: just like the old days of Sunday lunch.

And now it won't matter that today the sun did not

shine in the middle of July, because tomorrow it will be summer again – and after all, the roses need a rest from all that glare. And Felicity will stare out of the French windows at the back garden, where the rain is beginning at last to fall once more, like soft slow music starting up – a fine mist of rain so gentle you would not see it unless you looked quite hard, because now dusk is coming down anyway, on a day that never really got hold of the daylight properly at all, and only wants to retire, like someone with a touch of flu, back into the restful darkness.

Also by the same author

A critically-acclaimed poetry collection.

'It is a rare occurrence to find a new poet (or even an old one!) with such a command of both style and language, but Wigley is that uncommon thing.'

Claire Powell (*Planet*)

'Precise, unexpected and lyrical . . . the debut of an exceptionally gifted poet.' (Wayne Burrows)

'A very accomplished first collection.' (John Barnie)

£6.95   ISBN 1 84323 068 2